Heaven, Hell, or Houston

Thom Erb

For Shelly.

This book, or anything I've done thus far, could not have happened without your love and support. Your unending patience and understanding of the many hours lost while I've pursued my writing passion, as well as a myriad of other creative adventures, is so incredible to me. Thank you!

And always remember, that neither torrential rain, nor zombie apocalypse could ever keep me from you. There will never be enough words or enough books to dedicate to you for all your love and undying support. I love you!

This book is a homage, and a thank-you note to four of my favorite writers.

Thank you so much gents, your words have brought joy, fear, laughter, anger, excitement into my life. Oh, and not to mention, beyond a metric ton of inspiration and knowledge.

Joe R. Lansdale - The Outlaw, the Fighter, the Silent Teacher.
Elmore Leonard - The Voice, the Beat, the Groove.
Joe McKinney - The Lawman, the Guide, the Amigo.
Jonathan Maberry - The Warrior, the Sensei, the Friend.

"Gruesome and gritty action coupled with pulse-pounding horror. I couldn't put it down."

-David Dunwoody, author of EMPIRE and THE HARVEST CYCLE.

Thom Erb's HEAVEN, HELL, OR HOUSTON is feverish, hardscrabble Texas noir, with a salty mix of brooding revenge tale and literary grindhouse. Erb lends an authentic voice to a cast of rich but flawed characters, and a plot that promises action at every startling turn. A+++!

-Shroud Quarterly

"Erb delivers a dark and gritty zombie tale filled with wicked characters and gruesome violence and a cool-as-hell noir-like protagonist you can root for."

-David Bernstein, author of Machines of the Dead and Toxic Behemoth.

...The book you hold in your hands is something special: it is witness to a writer finding his center....Texas is a state of mind, and Thom Erb is ready to put you there. If you haven't read him before, you are in for a treat...
...Please, listen to him carefully.
Because once you do, you and I will share one of the most honest and sensitive Texas voices I have read outside of a Larry McMurtry novel.

-Joe McKinney, Multiple Bram Stoker Award Winner/Author of the Dead World Series.

Acknowledgement Page.

ZZ TOP- Every tormented step in in this book's creation, was kept in deep bluesy, gritty company by your deeply Texas rooted music.
BIG ERBAL THANK YOU!!!

Best Beta-Readers in the Erbal Universe. You guys rock!
Skip Novak, Sheldon Higdon, Kurt Criscione, Eric Ralston, Bridget Manns, Robin Casella, Stacy Gonzalez.
David Moody, David Bernstein, David Dunwoody, Michael Knost, Rick Hautala, Gord Rollo, Brian Keene, Gregory Hall, Charles Day, Joseph Mulak, Brady Allen, Scott Christian Carr, Ty Schwamberger, Dean Harrison, Lucy Snyder, Steven Shrewsbery, David Brockie, Nick Cato, Darren Gallagher, Lincoln Crisler, Alex Katrin, Michael Boatman, , Weston Ochse, TG Arsenault, Tony Trembly, William Cook, Tonia Brown, Adam Millard, James Roy Daley, Jackie and Dan Gamber, Louise Bohmer, Shannon Lee Simmons, Ben Eads, Jason Keene,
The Four Horsemen- Thank you so much for that very first beer and the safe space to lean on. Timothy Deal, Mark Wholley, Danny Evarts and Zjonny Morse.
The amazing Funky Werepig Radio Show- Friday's will always be party night.
The Marion Public Library- Tracy-Fleegel-Whitney. Support your local library folks.
Mucho Gracias to the mighty CITIZENS of the ERBAL NATION: Jerry and Marianne Gorman, Christine Gorman Sanchez, Paul Reynolds, Todd Housel, Darrell Sergent, Jeff Lewis, Ginger and Steve Hadden, Lisa Hornsby, Talana Erb Bruce Cramer, Diana Weber, Karl Weaver, Christine McCord, Marge Delmar, Gregg Deutschbein, Tim Deutschbein, Robert Cossaboon, Melani McWilliams, Todd Dykhuizen, Darrell Sergent, Jeff Casella, , Jim Briggs and Tammy Klaver, Amy Smith Hunter, Barbara Sergent.
The list grows on and on.

Foreword
By Joe McKinney

Texas is a land of legends.

The Lone Star State was carved out of rocks and swamps and forests and endless, endless deserts by outlaws and Tennessee deadbeat debtors and high society ladies; by Cherokees and hard charging lawmen; by Mexican migrant workers and billionaire oil men; all of them running from something, looking to start again.

Texas is the last, best chance for people of extraordinary character.

It's the home of musicians as diverse as Beyoncé and Buck Owens, Buddy Holly and Meat Loaf, Selena and ZZ Top. Writers like Sandra Cisneros, James Michener, Justin Cronin, Larry McMurtry, Katherine Anne Porter and Joe Lansdale, just to name a few, have all pulled their inspiration from under the wide Texas sky.

It is a land of dirt road small towns and snake-handling preachers, but also of vast cities of glass palaces where every taste, no matter how cosmopolitan, can find indulgence. It is a land of lonely highways that seem to stretch forever to the horizon, and of rocket ships that climb the highways of the sky toward a future we can only imagine.

Texas is a land defined by its vastness, its possibilities, its endless possibilities, yet that vastness hasn't driven Texans apart. Despite all the diversity, a unique voice, an attitude, has emerged that is uniquely Texan. It is more than style, more than an accent, more even than a jealously guarded pride in one's history and one's reputation among outsiders. Being a Texan, speaking with that voice, is an expression of one's character.

It can be imitated.

It can be emulated.

It can even be mocked.

But it can never be usurped by someone whose soul isn't Texan.

I believe that to the soles of boots.

And so, when I first got hold of the manuscript of the book you now hold in your hands, I thought: *Uh oh, this here's gonna be a problem.*

I thought there was no way that some guy from a little town in Wayne County, New York was going to pull off a story about a Texas Ranger, one of the proudest symbols of Texas independence and self-reliance, with any sort of conviction at all.

Then I read it.

And I'm here to tell you now that this book is damn good.

It's the story of a very bad man looking to extract his lethal revenge on the Texas Ranger who put him behind bars.

It's also the story of a road trip into the soul of a man battered time and again by bad circumstance and hard breaks, who nonetheless always seems to find just a little more inside himself to do the right thing, who can never simply *take the day off.*

And, oh yeah, it's got zombies too.

But above all, it has that unique, almost ineffable something that is uniquely Texan. Books like *Heaven, Hell or Houston* aren't accidents, I suspect. They are the products of a displaced soul. They are the products of a Texan, born elsewhere.

I myself was born in Cambridge, Massachusetts, so I get it.

But here's the thing.

The book you hold in your hands is something special: it is witness to a writer finding his center. If you are a stranger to the Erbal Universe, you will find instances of unspeakable cruelty here.

Turn back now if you have a weak constitution for such things.

There are moments in this book so offensive (especially to the father of young girls, like myself) they made my skin crawl. And then, and THEN, the author has the audacity to come back with a scene of brotherly forgiveness and understanding so deftly drawn that I couldn't help but put the book down, rest my chin on my chest, and get lost in thoughts of my own life, my own family.

Be prepared.

This is not a kind book. Rather, this is the kind of book that grabs you by the nuts and squeezes, all the while smiling at your surprise and pain.

There is an ocean of pain in these pages.

Yet, on the far side of that ocean, there is courage, and kindness, and ultimately, love.

This is not a horror story.

This is not a revenge story.

This is not a Grindhouse/family sit com mashup.

This is not even the story of a man in need of redemption, and ultimately finding, if not redemption, some kind of peace that leaves him the opportunity for goodness.

I'd call this book a collection of moral ambiguities.

A knot begging to be untied.

One doesn't simply live in Texas.

One IS Texas.

Texas is a state of mind, and Thom Erb is ready to put you there. If you haven't read him before, you are in for a treat.

Please, listen to him carefully.

Because once you do, you and I will share one of the most honest and sensitive Texas voices I have read outside of a Larry McMurtry novel.

Enjoy!

Joe McKinney
Helotes, TX
December 6, 2014

You may all go to Hell, and I will go to Texas.
Davy Crockett

1.

Jailhouse Rock
Oklahoma State Penitentiary
McAlester, Oklahoma
May 31, 1985
3:35 a.m.

The Voice shouted, implored in Isandro Dianira's twisted mind. Inmate #926934 smiled and reveled in the prison guard's warm blood, running over his scarred and calloused hands.

The Voice demanded blood. Isandro didn't think twice about shoving the shiv deep into the bitch's belly and was almost aroused at the thought of the dying man. He laughed as he let the guard's lifeless body fall like a discarded cigarette. He was the leader of *Los Malvados,* one of Mexico's more powerful gangs. The sweet smell of freedom was only a few seconds way. And after two years of intricate planning and a lot of cash spent, he'd kill his own brother to be on the outside. He crept down steel steps that led to the loading dock where, if all was going as planned, a garbage truck would be waiting for the most notorious cop killer in all Texas history.

The moon cast cold blue tinted shadows on the parking lot. Isandro leapt down into a crouch and waited for the signal. It should be one quick flash from a small penlight, followed by a short whistle. His thin, taut muscled body tensed in anticipation. Freedom was finally almost here, and he could taste it. But an even greater taste made his pulse quicken, vengeance.

He owed a certain Texas Ranger a special thank you for putting him in the Oklahoma State Prison on a ten-year stint. He had plans for piece of shit Texas Ranger, Jay McCutcheon. He

1

smiled as the small light flashed, and the whistle followed. The first cold rain drop hit him in the eye. He wiped it away and grinned as he spotted the large green garbage truck idling, while a stocky figure stood at the back end of it.

"Hector," Isandro said in a low voice and ran to his twin brother, hugging him "Great to see you, brother," Hector said, pushing Isandro toward the back.

"It's gonna get a bit...*dirty*, but the Crew are waiting on the outside. Hope you don't mind rolling around in shit for a few minutes, brother?" Hector said, trying to hug his brother again, but Isandro had enough of the touchy-feely bullshit already. He nodded coldly and grabbed a handle on the truck.

"Hell no. I've been rollin' in shit for the past two years. I can handle it." Isandro gave his brother's cheek a firm slap and hopped into the back of the truck. "Let's go."

Hector looked up. "What's the first thing you want to do?" he asked with a big grin.

"Puta" said Isandro, looking back up at the prison. "Then, I find McCutcheon and show him what pain and hell on Earth feels like." He spat on the rain-soaked pavement. "Vamanos!"

Isandro stared up at the black sky as rain attacked his cold, scarred face. He may be cold on the outside, but deep within, a roaring furnace of hate and revenge had been feverishly stoking for years. Now, he was free, and that meant the world was going to bleed.

2.

Good Texan
2700 feet above Dallas/Fort Worth International Airport
April 1, 1985
Friday, 8:30 p.m.

I wiped the sweat from my face and forced the bile from exploding out of my mouth. It tasted like stale enchiritos and boiled ass. The thought made me gulp another rush of burning liquid back down. Only about fifteen more minutes before I'd be off this shit-bird and headed home. That might just be about fourteen minutes too long, I feared. My stomach felt as if it were on a roller coaster designed by Satan himself. The plane ride from Washington had been painfully slow and torturous. The Governor had the personality of a dead tree stump. The cabin smelled like whiskey, cigars, and rot-ass farts. I'd been on babysitting duty for this ass-clown for only a few weeks and had already grown dead tired of all of his arrogant bullshit. But I couldn't decide which was worse, my hatred for flying, or the broken record of bad jokes the old gasbag spewed out like diarrhea through a lawn sprinkler.

"Say, son, did ya hear the one about the one legged spic and a jar of peanut butter?" The Governor laughed and punched my arm.

This guy's a real prize. I offered him a tight smile and pretended to give a rat's hairy ass..

This slimy politician had won the silver-spoon lottery and was a hell of a lot more crooked than the NFL, MLB, and the entire Congress combined. More bile mixed with spit. I choked it back, forced it down with a sip of water, and shot the portly man a passable look. I snatched the barf bag from the seat pouch in front of him. The fresh contents of the bag didn't help the back alley aroma of the plane. My gut rolled with the pitching plane.

"I hear ya got a hot little Mexican mamacita waitin' for ya when ass hits asphalt?" The Governor raised his long white, antennae-like eyebrows and gave me a lecherous wink.

"Yes, Sir. Her name's Inez. She's my fiancée." I had to keep cool. This guy was really starting to wear on my last nerve. I sipped on the warm water, hoping to get the puke taste from my mouth. Somehow, it was better tasting than the company I'd been stuck with for the past few hours. Don't get me wrong, I loved the job; being a Texas Ranger was all I ever wanted to be. It's a family legacy. From the very leafy-top of the McCutcheon family tree all the way on down to my middle-aged ass. We've all dedicated our lives; some even died for the Rangers. But hell, guard duty for this womanizing, crooked as a Sahuaro cactus tree on mescaline, was enough to test even the staunchest of diehard members of my family.

"Oh, now I don't mean no offense there, Ranger." The fat-ass in the wrinkled suit tapped me on the leg and shot another sickening wink.

"No offense taken, Sir." I swallowed, moving my leg out of his sweaty reach. I was never keen on lying and would prefer to throw the cuffs on this golden-tongue shit spinner, but knew all too well, where that would get me. I'd been down that road too many times to recall, and was pretty damn sure, this time, there would be no saving my career. And getting fired was not on my to-do list for the day. I chose to suck it up and wait for the damn plane to land.

"So, you have any pictures of this here fiancée of yours?" The old drunk nudged forward on his chair with a leathery squeak that sounded like he ripped a ripe one that would surely smoke out the entire cabin. He didn't even notice. I ignored the sound, but couldn't ignore the smell. Damn.

"Well, son, pics? Hold that thought. I need to take my lizard for a walk. Would ya mind fixin' me an Irish whiskey?" He shot me a wink and hoisted his fat ass out of the seat with another gaseous squeak.

"Oh, and a little splash of Tab too, if ya please." He slapped the small fridge with a chubby hand, and hurried back to the restroom, groping his crouch.

4

I thought the old man was a whole side of jackass, but I always followed orders and respected the position regardless of the pecker-head that held it. I took a deep breath, fetched a Lucky Strike from my inside breast pocket, and lit it. The soothing smoke filled my lungs as I walked to the small bar and began fixing the bat-shit crazy politician's goddamn whiskey—after I took a long swig for myself, of course.

I turned to Novak. "Jesus H. Christ. What did I ever do to deserve this living hell?" I walked to the bar and started to fetch the asshole's drink. "Can you believe this shit?" I whispered. All my partners had to offer were muffled laughs.

Assholes.

I guess I was more pissed off than I thought. As I turned toward my fellow Rangers, both shaking their heads, like they were on fire, and wore matching, mocking smiles. Higdon slowly mouthed the word, 'no,' over and over again. He knew me all too well. I looked down to see that I'd squeezed the Tab can and all its contents had spilled out onto the counter.

More laughter.

Fucking assholes.

"Oh, okay. Thanks, Mom." I snatched a towel, cleaned up my mess, and flipped them both the bird. I gave them a death stare as the plane made yet another not so subtle adjustment. My stomach was on fire.

The Governor stumbled back into the cabin with his hand out and a big cigar dangling from his thick lips. He snatched the glass from the bar, worked a zigzag dance to the chair, and promptly tumbled into it. The old professional didn't spill a drop or lose an ash.

"So Ranger, where were we? Oh yes. Do tell me about that sweet lil' mamacita ya got. Come on, show me something." The sloshed Governor sipped long from his glass, and the ice tumbled as he motioned with his cigar hand for me to ante up with some juicy details.

This was getting old. I washed the indignation down with another shot of whiskey I'd snatched from the bottle and wiped my mouth on the silk napkin from the side stand. *Okay you old Devil*

Dog, in a few hours, you'll be home, and your assignment with this fuck-knuckle will be over. Houston never sounded so good.

"C'mon now, son. I know you have to have some sexy Polaroid's or something. After all, you Rangers spend a lot of time away from home, and y'all must need some kind of spank material." Whiskey spilled from the drunk's mouth like a large mouth bass letting a tasty worm slip.

He had a reputation for ruining folk's careers. It seemed I always had one foot in the grave and the other on board a speeding freight train hell bent for leather, 120 miles an hour, in the opposite direction. I didn't have a lot of room for forgiveness. Inez and me having a little girl, Bellia, a new house and a wedding to pay for, the last thing I needed to do was piss this perverted old man off and become the next on his kill list. Hell, that and being about thirty minutes from a two week vacation, I reluctantly pulled my wallet from my back pocket and flipped it open to Inez's photo.

The chubby hands of the Governor flashed out, snatched the wallet from hands, and brought the photo to his wide eyes.

"Well, sweet Jesus, Ranger. Holeeee sheeeit." The Governor slunk back into his chair. His eyes stuck wide open, and his thick cigar-stained tongue licked at his even fatter lips like a snake tasting the air.

My jaw muscles tightened into knots, and my fists clenched. I hated politics and all the evil leeches it spawned. Now I had a fitting face for the dirty stereotype. *Only a few more minutes until we land,* I tried to convince myself.

I could see Novak and Higdon gauging my reaction, and they tensed for what might be the latest in what they so laughingly termed, *McCutcheon's Fist-of Follies,* or my latest fuck up. They'd served with me a long time and knew. However, my career was far more important than letting this pig, or my overactive demons, get the best of me.

Attention: We are about to make our approach to land. So, please be seated everyone and make sure to fasten your seat belts. The Captain's smooth voice crackled over the speakers of the tension-filled cabin.

"Well, Jesus Christ ridin' in a sidecar ridin' down Main Street. She is one hot piece of ass y'all got there, son." The old man grabbed his crotch, and his tongue lapped the air. His grin looked like it could swallow the entire wallet. His cackle turned into a smoker's cough.

White rage exploded inside me. I took one-step toward the gaped-mouth politician, but halted as my partners matched my movement. "Old bastard is about to resign from office, involuntarily!" I murmured through clinched teeth.

"Take it easy, cowboy. Keep it in your pants. I'm just sayin' your wife-to-be is one beautiful lady." The fat letch held up his chubby hand in a halt motion. He flashed a sleazy smile. I wanted to knock his dentures down his whiskey-soaked throat, but stayed put.

"Yes. She...is. Thank...thank you, Sir." I forced the words through pursed lips. Again, my partners watched me liked overprotective nannies.

"I do have to ask, son, does her pussy taste as sweet as she looks?" The lecherous pig's tongue jutted out, licked the photo, and grunted as he held it to his slobbering face.

In a flash that even surprised the other Rangers, I lunged and slugged the horned up old man in the jaw, sending him rolling out of his chair and sprawling onto the carpeted floor. I saw Higdon rushing to the Governor's side, while Novak pulled me off and slammed me into the wall. In my rage, I fought back, but Novak had a good fifty pounds on me. The shots of Jameson played into the big man's favor as well. He was too strong and pinned me down. We'd have a *conversation* about this later.

"Chill out, Jay. You don't need this shit-storm," Novak whispered into my ear. I stared at the bleeding piece of trash on the floor. I really wanted to kill the bastard. I knew my partner was right. The jerk was always right. I relaxed and dropped my arms. The big Ranger lessened his grip, but didn't let go completely.

"You cool?" Novak asked. His intense brown eyes stared at me, making sure I understood. He wasn't just pissing in the wind.

"Yeah. I'm cool." I nodded. We both knew I was lying.

Attention: Take your seats y'all. I'm not sure what's going on back there, but we are about to land, so I suggest y'all take your seats. The Captain's irate tone broke the volatile silence.

"Good idea. Governor, let me help you up, Sir." Higdon tried to help the drunken man up.

"Piss off. I can get up myself, for Christ's sake. I ain't no damn cripple," the Governor shouted, and dabbed a handkerchief across his bloody maw. He pushed away the offer for help and struggled back into his leather chair, now covered in whiskey. He tried to straighten his suit and save some dignity, but lost horribly on both accounts. His erection was still standing at attention as he continued to wipe his blubbery face. He shot me a dirty look. A look I'd seen far too often.

After a few heated moments, they were all buckled in and waiting for the plane to make its descent onto the runway. I sat there, and the reality began to hit me. I screwed up for the last time. That was it. No job. No wedding, and no honeymoon.... No goddamn career. What was I going to tell Inez? She would leave me for sure this time and take Bellia with her. I'd be alone...again. And damn well deserve it.

After the San Antonio and Galveston fiascos, I was damn lucky she stayed with my sorry ass that long. I couldn't lose her and the baby. There's no way in hell I could live without them. I might as well be dead. At this point, with the federal life insurance and pension, I was worth a hell of a lot more dead than alive. The option was never far from my mind.

I wasn't ready to give up just yet. I swallowed hard and looked over at the twitching bastard, taking a deep breath.

"Sir, I want to apolo—"

"Save it, boy! You fucked with the wrong hombre, my friend." The old man held up a hand and wouldn't even look in my direction.

Novak, and Higdon, both gave exasperated, apologetic frowns toward me. It didn't make me feel any better.

"Fuck me running!" I repeated as the small plane made its final decent into the Airport. My stomach and future sank the closer the plane neared the warm, wet pavement.

3.

I'm Bad, I'm Nationwide
Rt. 45 South, Oklahoma
Friday, 8:53 p.m.

The Cadillac roared down the slick road, whipping past trees and telephone poles like they stood still. They'd stopped for gas and more booze at a small town Stop-N-Rob and acquired more than alcohol.

"What's the word on the puta, McCutchon?" Isandro asked, sipping from a bottle, and rubbing the top of a blonde girl's head.

"No offense, Boss, but why you have such a hard-on for this guy?" Cahill asked.

The rest of the crew fell silent and stared out the windows. Even Bobby and Manny, who were in the middle of molesting a young bleach-blonde dressed in a high school cheerleader uniform.

"Who the fuck is the pasty-ass, white bread puta?" Isandro held his thin, muscular arms out wide and looked deeply for an answer.

"Hey brother, he's new. He don't know what's goin' on," Hector abruptly said from the driver's seat.

"Yeah, he's cool, Boss," Manny added. "Just stupid is all." They all laughed, and Isandro shot the thin white boy a long, cold stare.

"Sorry…Boss. I was just wond…"

Isandro stared with a fiery glare at the shaking white boy. "They fuckin' set me up, esé, if ya must know." Isandro leaned against the backseat of the big Cadillac, while the girl forcibly serviced him.

"Him and that bitch of a District Attorney." Isandro felt the rage welling up inside him. He took a long drink, but it did little to calm the fire that licked his insides. He knew he was guilty of every charge and even many more that no one knew about. But he would not be controlled or punished by anyone, especially the white law pigs and the traders such as the bitch DA that helped to extradite him for the six cases of murder back in Oklahoma.

Both of those motherfuckers would die painful, slow death. Isandro's grim vow was the only thing that got the brutal killer through each hellish day in the hole.

"The bastard is hard to find. We spent some cake and fount out he's shacked up somewhere in Houston, but that's as far as we got. But, we found him. You'll love this, homes." Manny chuckled and let white plumes of smoke out with each wheeze. "He's gettin' married and has a fuckin' kid." The young banger's shaggy hair covered his bloodshot eyes.

"Oh, hell no." Isandro laughed, his hand gripping tighter on the girl's head. He sipped from the bottle and looked out the window at the rain pelting the glass.

"I shit you not. And you'll never guess who that pussy is getting married to?" Manny took a long drag from the joint, nodding with an illegal smile a mile wide.

"Who?" Isandro rubbed the girl's head as she continued to blow him. He ignored her sobs and cries for mercy. With a wicked smile, he quickly yanked her hair back.

Manny and the others laughed. "That Santana bitch, esé."

"Merry fucking Christmas to me," he stated coldly.

The rest of the crew nodded and smiled with their boss.

"McCutcheon, and that bitch DA, are tying the fuckin' knot?" Isandro slammed the girl's face down on his member and bellowed a laugh that terrified everyone inside the speeding Caddy.

"It's true, brother," Hector hesitantly spoke up from the driver's seat. The rest of the crew followed his lead and the car erupted with raucous laughter and calls for more booze and bloody, violent revenge.

"Conchetumare!"

10

Isandro slapped the white girl blowing him in the back of the head. "Watch your fuckin' teeth, puta," He howled as the skunky pot smoke rolled from his mouth.

The girl's terrified sobs and cries for help fell on deaf ears and only received a devilish grin from Isandro. His cold black eyes stared at the trembling girl. He tilted his head with dark curiosity.

"I didn't say stop. Suck my dick or suck this." He shoved the barrel of the .357 into her quivering mouth. The convertible filled with drunken, drug-induced laughter as the terrified girl, who's college ID said was twenty, but she didn't look was lucky if she was a split-second over the age of sixteen, deep throated the big gun. Isandro liked that. She quickly took the stocky Mexican's member back into her bleeding mouth, and her tears helped lubricate the blowjob.

"See, you just need to know how to train these putas." Isandro yanked the girl's hair, and he laughed as she whimpered. He took a swig from the Tequila bottle and poured it over the crying girls head. The laughter only got louder. It had been a long 72 hours and much blood had been shed and lives lost, but Isandro thrived on that shit—lived for it. And the more mayhem and chaos he created, the harder his dick got, and the darker his aspirations became. The bloody trail of carnage began in McAlester, Oklahoma, and only grew more brutal and deadlier the farther along he and his circus of drug-induced insanity traveled.

"Can ya save some of that tasty ass for me this time, Issie?" Cahill begged from the front seat.

Isandro glared at the punk. "Wait your fuckin' turn, bitch. Besides, she's too fine to waste on your pasty-white ass."

"Ah, hell, nah...man." drool slipped from Cahill's slack mouth onto the leather seat as he rubbed the small aching in his worn, blood stained Wranglers.

"Keep that shit to yourself, man." Isandro glared, trying to ignore the kid.

The night sped by like a movie in fast forward as the angry Mexican spilled his load inside the terrified teenager's mouth. He pushed her toward his anxious flunky and wiped his cock in her hair. He took a sip from the bottle as he shoved his prick back into his pants. He owned the world, and he planned to rape it of all he could. Breaking out of prison wasn't easy. When you are part of one of the most powerful gangs in the country, if not the world, you can get away with shit like that.

Isandro lost track of the mangled bodies he left in his wake. He didn't give a shit either way. He had spent nine hard years in an Oklahoma prison and only had one thing on his mind. Well, maybe more than one. You can only fuck and drink enough before that gets old. No, his sights were set on Mexico. His family was there, waiting. He had missed most of his kids' lives, and he wasn't wasting any more time. He didn't care how many cops or innocents he had to kill to get there. He was going to take what was coming to him...

Freedom.

He was damn tired of being the world's bitch. He had taken the fall for the Crew, and he was damn proud to do so. There were far too many pussy's running the show down in Mexico. They all needed a kick in the ass. If that didn't work, a bullet to the bean would train them pendejos damn quick. He took a swig from the bottle of Tequila and watched as the twitchy white boy and Manny took turns pounding the young white girl. It made him laugh as she cried out for help through a spit, blood covered mouth. It made his dick twitch and made him think about sticking it in her ass one last time. However, the sudden need to piss washed that urge away.

"Hector, pull over man. I need to piss," he ordered.

"Got it, el hermano." Isandro's twin nodded from the driver seat.

The old Cadillac veered off the rain-soaked road and pulled in behind a closed McDonald's. The steam rose off the hot pavement like a steak sizzling on a grill. The moon was soft and glowed an anemic yellow as the big car came to a stop behind the overfilled dumpster. The strains of Mariachi music bounced off the clay red, yellow, and white bricks of the fast food joint and the dumpster as Isandro staggered out of the back seat. In one hand, he held his stiff prick, and in the other, his loaded revolver. He looked ready to use both.

Groans of orgasm followed Isandro as he found a place to let his piss flow and have a break from the rutting hogs in the Caddy. He leaned against the rusty blue dumpster, and even his piss fled his body with anger. He was once a kid on the streets who loved to help the old women of the town and all that shit, but once you get stabbed and shot a few times by so-called 'family,' you learn fucking quick that trust is hard to come by. That very thought had helped him carve his way from Oklahoma to this shitty, rain soaked parking lot, filled with used rubbers and dirty heroin needles.

The light from the Caddy's headlights danced across the sparkling broken glass blacktop. He motioned with the pistol, and Hector knew exactly what he meant. The rain poured down and danced as Isandro's goons yanked the young blond girl from the idling car. She screamed and pleaded for help, but the raging thunderstorm, and the Mexican gangster's lack of giving a fuck, washed it all away like the early spring's torrents. Two of his crew threw the hysterical girl onto the yellowing blacktop in front of their boss, who was rubbing the revolver against his stained zipper.

"Please…. don't," the blonde quivered.

"Don't what?" Isandro knelt down.

'I…I did everything you wanted. Please don't…"

"Bitch, you keep sayin' don't, so what the fuck do you NOT want me to do?" Isandro smashed the bottle over her shivering head, and her blood instantly mixed with the pouring rain. He stood and put the large revolver to her sobbing head. The cheerful mariachi music and raging storm almost washed away the gunshot that sent the girl's brains across McDonald's empty parking lot.

"Hector, let's get the fuck outta here," Isandro said. The girl still lay twitching on the cold pavement, as he got back into the Caddy and slammed the door.

"Next?" Isandro said.

4.

Going So Good

Dallas/Fort Worth International Airport Parking Garage
Friday, 9:01 p.m.

The landing and uncomfortable disembarking was the longest thirty minutes of my sad life. The Governor finished the bottle of whiskey as we waited to land, and I knew damn well there was no talking my way out of this one. Part of me knew the sick bastard had it coming and didn't feel bad about knocking him on his old ass. In fact, I wished my partners would've let me finish the job. That was what my therapist called my 'self-destructive rage' pouring out. Fuck that overpriced money grabber and her damn labels. I chewed on that thought as we made our way to the long black limousine idling at the level A Concourse.

The long concrete hallway funneled us toward the awaiting car. My chest squeezed like a vice, and my stomach wanted to burst out through my goddamned belly button. I had to try one last time to save my career; ah, who was I kidding? My entire damn life. The Governor was about to enter the limousine as I rushed past Novak, who tried to stop me, but I jerked my arm away. I grabbed the door before one of the Governor's aides could close it, and put myself between the door and the old man.

"Governor, I just need a second. I cannot tell you just how sorry I am for overreacting the way I did. I was way out of line. Will you please just let me explain myself?" I spat out in one breath, and inside, prayed to a God I'd never had known, and up until this very moment, didn't give two-shits to know. Now...I was beginning to believe. At least, pretended to. I swallowed hard and stared into the drunken politician's unblinking eyes. The Governor waved the driver to hold for a moment, turned back to me, and just stared, silently, impatiently waiting for my groveling to begin.

The storm clouds that had followed the plane from D.C. took up staunch residence over the cold airport and shut out any possible light the moon tried to offer. I took a deep breath, and could see my partners off to the left, as I turned to the irritated Governor, who was pouring a drink inside the limo.

"Sir, see, my wedding is in two days. Inez, my fiancée, has me all stressed out with all the planning. We've been on duty for over 72 hours with minimal sleep. I know that's no excuse for hitting you, Sir. I...I just snapped," I said, as a cold wind whisked down into the cement tunnel of the garage.

The old man didn't seem impressed and glared at me, sipped at his whiskey, and leaned back into the leather seats.

"Sir, Ranger McCutcheon is a highly decorated officer, and he really—" Novak interjected, and the Governor waved him off.

"I am well aware of Ranger McCutcheon's so-called service record. It seems I wasn't the first victim of your anger, was I, son?" The Governor continued to stare at me, and a slight smirk appeared on the old man's weather worn face. That just fueled rage, and I was about ten seconds from pouring the old man's face across the expensive leather. But I again prayed to any damned God that would listen. The incidents the drunken governor was talking about were many, but all were justified, at least to me. Besides, they were a long time ago, and I was a changed man now. Hell, I was a work in progress. The brisk motion to the driver from the placid Governor stopped my bad memories.

"But Sir, please." I reached out and grabbed the man's sleeve of his wool coat and was met with a glare of contempt.

"Sir, I...I be...beg of you. I will lose my job. You will end my career. Can you please?" I felt the honest tears slipping from my usually tight, denying tear ducts, but knew it was all I had left in the tank.

The Governor's fat face turned into a slab of granite and stared out the front of the idling limousine. He held up a pudgy palm in my face. I choked back tears.

"There is nothing I can do for you, son. I will be speaking to your superiors in the morning, and I will be asking for your badge." Just then the dark sky opened up and cold rain fell from it like an ebony piñata.

"But, Sir," I shouted, as the sudden rain soaked us all to the bone in mere seconds. Steam rolled off the pavement, creating a ghostly haze in the parking garage.

The Governor motioned for me to come close, and he responded.

"I wouldn't do anything for a piece of cow shit like you even if I could. However, I just wanted you to know, your soon to be wife is a hot piece of ass, and when I jerk off tonight, it will be her face I see when I spew my juice." The Governor winked, smiled wide, and shoved his clammy palm into my face, laughing as an aide closed the door.

A flurry of lightning strikes washed out the black Lubbock skyline, leaving me rain-soaked in a tear-filled rage as the limousine drove out into the night. I was damned sure my future went speeding away with it. I needed to get home, back to Houston.

"I'm so sorry, Jay. I—" Novak offered, but I didn't want to hear it.

I stalked off into the darkness of the parking garage and several ball-shaking rounds of thunder ushered my exit.

I could sense Higdon and Novak's eyes following me, and I felt like shit blowing them off. They were good Rangers and even better friends. Better than I deserved, and I am well aware of how my chaotic reputation as, Texas Ranger James Mathew McCutcheon, one of the best ever to wear the badge, was also known as one of the most violent. The dumb-asses would both be praying, maybe to the same God that ignored me earlier, that I would just keep my mouth shut, turn tail and go home to Inez. Instead of doing something really stupid.

My partners knew their prayers were like pissing in the Grande Canyon. It was a waste of time. A loud squawking came over the airport speakers. Something about an emergency, but I had my own shit to deal with. I stalked away as the rain intensified and turned a sickly shade of yellow.

5.

Decision or Collision
Dallas/Ft. Worth International Airport Parking garage
Friday, 9:14 p.m.

I turned the key to my 1969 Plymouth Barracuda. It roared to life as I lit the Lucky Strike and fetched the flask of Jim Beam from the glove box. A barrage of thunder and crackling lightning fought to drown out my anger, but failed. My body shook with rage, and I inhaled the cigarette in what seemed like a matter of seconds before realizing I had lit the second. My mind swirled with a flurry of emotions and manic thoughts. Several dark, frantic moments passed before I made a decision.

I sipped slowly at the flask. It was my only tangible family McCutcheon heirloom. My great grandfather brought it home from his service days in WWI. I ran my thumb over the deep indentation, where rumored had it, a pissed off French husband had shot my grandfather for liberating his wife from her panties. Another charming trait handed down through the twisted generations. I sipped and thought how many drunken McCutcheon men had sat and drank from this rugged steel flask.

"Thanks, assholes," I said aloud and pulled two photo down from the visor. Tears formed in my weary eyes. One, was taken the night we got engaged. We'd made the trip down to Inez folks' house in Saltillo. It was such a great time. I sipped again and stared at the second photo. It was at Bellia's Christening. She and her mother were so beautiful. Little Bellia with her soft head of dark hair. Thank God, she looks like her mamacita; I half chuckled, half cried.

The past year had been a dark blur, and after all the shit, I was damn lucky Inez had stayed with me. The shooting and the accident took their toll on me and my family. The heavy thought of the recent events with the Governor only served to remind me that my luck was about to run out, and that I had pretty much sealed my fate with Inez. This was going to be too much. The warm whiskey slid down my throat. How could I have fucked up again? Christ, I'd been asking myself that question a lot over the past few years, and the answer never came. I had a feeling the damn flask would be empty by the time I got out of the godforsaken parking garage.

The Allman Brothers, *"Ain't Wastin' Time No More,"* rolled out through the tape deck and my harried mind cleared. I suddenly realized that whatever God I had prayed to, had finally answered my pleas, and this was a sign. I tossed out the spent cigarette and took a sip from the flask, chucked it back into the glove box, and put the Hearst shifter into drive

The rain pelted the midnight blue Plymouth as it made its way out the airport-parking garage and turned onto the freeway heading southeast.

I had made my decision. The rainstorm followed behind me as I made my way toward Houston.

6.

Just Got Paid
RT. 45 South

The wet road hissed underneath the tires of the Cadillac and a sign that read: 'Welcome to Texas,' passed by in the cool night. No one inside the car noticed or cared. Gray smoke poured out the tinted windows and mixed with the steam rolling off highway 45. Sporadic street lights flickered as they rushed by, but Isandro wasn't fazed or even bothered to notice.

"Hey esé, we are all out of cervezas and Tequila. We gotta find a store pronto, yo," Isandro ordered. The car had been quiet since they got rid of the 'party favor.' He felt this tour of chaos needed a push and running out of liquor was not the way to do it. He downed the last of the Tequila and the weed was almost all smoked. *That shit ain't gonna fly,* he told himself.

He kept staring at the photo of his twins and fought with every ounce from crying. He could not afford to show his crew any sign of weakness. That was what had landed his ass in jail the last time, and he swore, once he slit the guard's throat and hid inside the garbage truck, that he would never, ever, be fucking weak again— even if it killed him. Being dead is better than being a gutless puta.

"I think I see a sign for a liquor store," Hector said, turning on his right signal and heading down the off ramp for the neon salvation in the wet and cold Texas night.

A solitary, small yellow light hung over the cracked pavement of the old liquor store like a dying flower on a vine. A fine mustard colored rain painted the porous black top as the Caddy screeched to a stop in front of the store. The worn wipers fought to clear the slimy rain from the windshield and a cold wind came out of the north. Isandro shivered as he crawled out the back seat. The rest of his crew followed, save Hector, who stayed behind the wheel of the humming Caddy.

Isandro scanned the rain soaked lot and spotted a rusty red Chevy pick-up and blue Ford Torino station wagon. Inside the wagon, a frantic woman scolded two young children. He took note and headed inside the liquor store. The warning sound of jingle bells rang as they walked into the well-stocked store. The sea of bottles looked like liquid salvation to Isandro, and he surveyed the booze-lined walls.

"Be cool," Isandro whispered to his goons, as they spread out across the store; each knew their jobs and what would happen to their sorry asses if they screwed up. The brain-splattered blonde back at Mickey Dee's was a clear example of what happens when *Big Papi* is pissed. They didn't want any of that shit. Fuck that noise.

***

Paul Reynolds was dog-tired. The swing shift at the plant was killing him, and he really needed some vodka. Something, anything that would numb him from the shit-hole that his life had become since he knocked up that bitch Traci. God surely must have really been pissed at his sorry ass when he blessed him with not just one, but two know-it-all teenage brats. Once he had dreams of being the next quarterback for the Dallas Cowboys, now, hell, he slaves his shit-ass life away at the oil refinery and just waits impatiently for liver failure to take him away from his hell on Earth. "Not soon enough," he cursed as he snatched a bottle of Mad Dog 20/20 from the crowded shelf and shoved it into his worn jacket. He hoped the old man at the counter wasn't watching. That was the last thing he needed. He just wanted to get shit-faced drunk and forget about his life. Watch the Rangers on their crappy T.V. and sleep all weekend. Maybe jerk off while watching the Solid Gold Dancers, then lapse into after orgasmic coma, and pray that death would come calling before Monday morning.

Little did he know his prayer would soon be answered.

***

The last thing that went through Paul's mind was the ringing of the jingle bells on the liquor store door and the 9mm round that splattered his brain matter and blood over the Capt. Morgan display. Cahill held the smoking gun and laughed like a sick hyena.

Isandro grabbed Cahill by the head and slammed his thin frame into a wall of gin bottles. The glass shattered, sending the clear liquid splashing all over them both. He swung the pistol into Cahill's temple, slicing his head open, and the young kid slid down the shattered shelf full of broken glass and dripping gin.

"You stupid pendejo. What the fuck you thinkin', esé?" Isandro emphasized his displeasure with a work boot to the kid's stomach. He could see movement from behind the counter and bolted for it.

"Be cool, Pops." Isandro buried the pistol's muzzle into the owner's old face, shoving him back into the bottles of liquor behind the counter. "And I won't have to do you like that maricón." The pistol directed the old man's bifocal eyes to the twitching man on the matted brown carpet.

"Uhm...o...okay. I...I'm cool." The old man shook and winced as Isandro pressed the barrel of the Beretta into the man's sweat-covered forehead. Isandro grinned as he caught a tear rolling down the man's craggy cheek.

"Good, Gramps, good." He lowered the gun and looked at the rest of his crew. They all just stood there staring at Cahill's limp body.

"Yo, putas. Time to go shoppin'. Papi is thirsty." He laughed and walked to the old man behind the counter. He shoved the old man down to his shaking knees and smiled.

"Make it quick, vatos, because of puta's fuck up we need to get the fuck outta here." He knelt next to the crying man, patted him on the white, balding head, and watched on as the crew filled plastic shopping bags with his preferred alcohol. He watched Cahill lie in a booze-soaked and bloody heap on the floor. Isandro laughed. He liked kicking the shit out of the white boy. He needed to send a clear message, and the last thing he needed to do was let this puta act out of orders. After all, he would do the killing. Isandro had a number in his head, and that number hadn't been reached yet. He almost felt bad for the poor putas that were in his way. But that passed pretty damn quickly.

He rubbed the old man's shoulders as the crew resupplied and offered comforting words in Spanish. The old man even leaned into him and stopped crying.

"Yo mataria tu," Isandro cooed and kissed the man on the head, as the crew finished up and headed for the door. Apparently, the old man spoke Spanish, because he tried to crawl away sobbing.

"Noooo!" the old man begged.

"To the car, now!" Isandro didn't look at the crew and raised the gun at the old man trying to get away on the bloodstained carpet.

Gunshots rang out into the dark night of the parking lot. Isandro dragged Cahill by the gin and blood-soaked jacket and tossed him down in front of the Caddy. He looked around. Movement inside the Torino caught his cold eyes. He looked at Bobby and Manny, and then pointed to the blue Ford. They shoved the bags of booze into the Caddy and pulled their pistols, sprinting to the car.

The cold rain pelted the blacktop so fierce that it almost blotted out the yellow lights above them. Isandro approached the car with pistol raised. He nodded for others to flank the car on either side. He waited for his goons to get in place and then yanked the driver side door open. It creaked and triggered a dog to bark somewhere off in the dark night.

The rain intensified, almost obscuring the dome light inside. Manny must have seen movement; the car lit up with his pistol's muzzle flash. The windshield splattered with deep red and brain matter as frantic screams escaped from the back seat, adding another dog to the evening choir.

Isandro snatched the backdoor and shoved his pistol inside. This time the yellow glow of the dome light worked just fine. He nodded his head and smiled at the occupants of the Gran Torino's backseat.

"Buenos, hola, buenas tardes señoritas." Isandro bowed and winked at the two beautiful teen girls, trembling in hysterics in the glow of the dome light. He motioned with the gun. The two goons whipped open the door on the other side, and dragged them kicking and screaming out onto the soaked parking lot.

Isandro walked to them and felt his crotch squirm as he estimated they were about high school age. "Just about right," he said, as he knelt down and yanked one of the blonde haired girl's head back. Rain splattered on a fear-filled face and mixed with her tears. His crotch twitched more.

"Ésta perras jóvenes bien en el coche," he ordered, and gave the panicked girl a deep tongue kiss. It muffled her screams.

He smiled and let loose the girl's long hair. "Wanna go for a ride, ladies?" He stood, not trying to hide his large erection. Their screams set off a half dozen more neighborhood dogs to bay into the cold rainy night.

"Oh, I don't think your parents will mind." turning on his booted heel, Isandro slowly sauntered to the car. He laugh at the sight of whimpering young captives.

Isandro had only just begun. There were many miles from here to Mexico, and he prayed he had enough bullets. He was sure as hell that there would be plenty of booze.

7.

Waitin' for the Bus
On board Greyhound bus 67 from Rochester, NY to Dallas, Texas
7:15 p.m.

Stacy Jo Casillas was a runner. She always had been. She ran away from her Podunk hometown of Arcadia Falls. She left behind an abusive, drunk father and a future that offered her nothing but an abusive husband and popping out babies like a Pez dispenser on speed. She had other plans with her life, and she sure as hell wasn't going to stick around to be some kind of sick replacement wife for her father after the real one split with the mailman. Her life was an actual punch line and this bitter sixteen year old was having no part of it. She worked part time at Somerville Drug store over the winter, saved her money, and bought a ticket. She considered it her lottery ticket because she was winning a new life and freedom—something she had never known.

She had hitched a ride to Rochester, where she boarded a bus and headed south. It was a long and boring ride. She needed to get stoned, badly. She couldn't think of any better time than now. There were a couple of creepy old men that kept eyeing her up and down. The skeevy pervs didn't scare her, but her stranger danger was on high alert. She had stolen her father's Buck knife and knew how to use it. At least she hoped she had.

The rain began as the bus hit the Texas border and hadn't stopped. Bright flashes of white lightning lit the dark bus and made the already ugly riders even uglier and scarier. Her ticket was for Houston, but an aching in her stomach told her she needed to get off the bus at the next stop. The fat guy with the Coke-bottle glasses kept slowly moving seats to get closer to her. She may have grown up in a farm town, but her tough as nails Puerto Rican Papi taught her how to fight and survive. She wasn't afraid to do just that, but she was trying to get away from that whole life. So, she figured better flight than fight.

The drumming rain filled the bus with a thunderous pounding sound that drowned out Prince's, *"Purple Rain,"* on her Walkman. Stacy Jo saw the fat guy now, only two rows away, and ogling at her like she was a Big Mac with a large fry. A bright flash illuminated his pudgy face, and his eyes seemed to glow in the bluish light.

The bus driver's voice squawked over the cracked speakers. *"Ten minutes until the next stop, folks."*

This was her chance to avoid sickos and to *light the fires*, as she liked to refer to pot smoking therapy. She got up and went into the tiny bathroom at the back of the bus. It smelled as if everyone on the bus used the floor and sink instead of the cramped crapper. The bus jostled as she shut the sticky door. The light inside flickered and refused to stay on full time. Its odd time flashes almost gave her an instant migraine, but she would take that over being the next girl on the pervert's jerk off reel. The bus rocked, and a drum roll of thunder accompanied the rain pelting down. She reached into her backpack and made sure the Buck knife was still there. A sigh of relief followed when her thin hand found it. She pulled out the small metal bowl a guy friend of hers in school made in machine shop. A pounding on the door, jolted her. She to dropped the bowl back into the backpack, as thunder rocked the bus.

"Occupied," Stacy Jo shouted over the raging storm. She pushed against the bi-fold doors and reached for her bag with the other.

"I gotta piss, girl. Let me in," the herky-jerky, high-pitched voice clamored through the thin door. The door shook with the pounding from the other side, and Stacy Jo's heart began to pound.

"I fucking said, *OCCUPIED, ASSHOLE!*" she shouted, and leaned into the buckling door, frantically reaching for her bag. The bus took a sharp left curve, and the door crashed open under the massive weight of the fat guy from two rows over. He grunted as he slammed into Stacy Jo, and his chubby hands pawed at her as he pinned her against the back wall of the small bathroom. She tried to push his big frame off, but he was too big. She punched and kicked, but the blows hitting his big body had no effect. He just laughed, grabbed her breasts, and tried to shove his hand down her pants.

"Come on, baby. I seen you watching me since Pittsburgh." His thick tongue flicked at her ear as she fought to push him off. The bouncing of the bus only helped the fat man as he put his full weight against her, tearing at her father's Army jacket, and her jeans. He ripped her t-shirt, exposing her bra. She felt his hot saliva roll down her cheek and onto her chest.

"Get the fuck off." She fell down onto the toilet seat, bringing her closer to her bag. He chortled and grunted like a pig in heat. She could feel his hard-on against her chest as she punched his fat gut and reached into her bag.

"Ya know you been wanting me, baby. Don't fight it." He drooled in her ear and grabbed her small tits. The bus rolled and sent the big man slamming against the thin doors. She acted fast, pulled the Buck knife from its sheath inside her orange and black backpack, and held it out in front of her.

"Back off, asshole," she shouted. Her voice, lost amongst the roar of the diesel engine, and the raging storm outside the speeding bus.

"Play nice, kitten. I only want a taste." The fat man wiped the drool from his bouncing jowls and lunged at her.

His eyes grew wide and mouth went slack as she felt the knife pierce deep into the man's rotund stomach. Hot blood spilled over her hand, and she heard the fat man asking for his Mommy as he slid down and crumpled into the small space of the bathroom.

The lights flickered, reminding her of an old black and white movie as she stared at the rich crimson blood dripping from her knife, and the fat man dying at her feet. The rain was unrelenting, and thunder seemed to not want to be far behind. The fat man cried and stared up at her as his last breath escaped from his spit-covered face. He pulled at her pant leg, begging for his Mommy. His last wish was left unfulfilled. Stacy Jo wiped the big man's blood on his sweat-stained t-shirt and left the bathroom.

The bus driver came over the speakers: "*We've arrived at Moe Whiskey's Horseshoe Lounge and Bus Station - Best damn Bar-BQ this side of the Mississippi. So I hope you're hungry.*"

Stacy Jo grabbed her gear and tried to hide the blood on her hands as she stepped off the dark Greyhound.

8.

Que Lastima
Rt. 45 South, Texas
Friday, 9:40 p.m.

The rain turned cold—cold enough for me to turn the car's heater on. The windows began to fog, and the last blinding effect I needed was a ghostlike haze blurring my vision. The whiskey was doing a fine enough job of that on its own. The windshield wipers slapped to Willie Nelson's, *"It's Cryin' Time Again,"* and almost drove my eyelids to close before a blaring horn from a tractor-trailer shook me upright. The rumble strips on the shoulder was a second reminder that if I wasn't careful, I'd get in a wreck. That was all I needed to end this shit-full day. I jolted the steering wheel, fought to right the 'Cuda, and exhaled as I centered the car between the lines.

A strong wind pushed the Plymouth, and a photo from the visor fell onto my lap, as lightning flashed across the Texas night. I snatched it up and looked at it. The car swerved as another gust of wind punched at it.

I pulled over onto the soft shoulder and slammed the transmission into park. My arms flailed for purchase on the photo. Once found, I held it to my chest and fought the tears away. I leaned over, opened up the glove compartment, pulled a bottle out, leaned back, and exhaled. After a long pull, my breathing calmed, and all I could do was stare at the photo.

"I'm so sorry." Tears flowed down, like the cold torrent outside the rumbling Plymouth. I shook with desperation as the odd, yellowish rain fell around the parked car. I wasn't going to make Houston tonight, and to even try would be sure suicide. Not that suicide wasn't a bad option at this shitty point in my life, but my better angels won out. I decided to stop for a bit, maybe grab some chow and a quick nap.

I kissed the photo, shoved it into my shirt pocket, put the car in gear, and pulled back onto the slick road. The big tires spat gravel as the 'Cuda headed south, and I looked for a good place to rest for the night.

Any neon sign offering booze would do the trick, besides, something told me Inez wouldn't be home when I got there anyway. I found the bottle on the seat and drank from it. Drained it and chucked it onto the backseat floor. It clunked against the other empties. Now, I really needed to find a bar.

Here I was, James Mathew McCutcheon, Texas Ranger, big bad-ass, Marine Recon, hard as steel warrior, far weaker than I ever showed or had the balls to admit. A hard lesson learned from James McCutcheon Senior. I still had the scars to remind me of the harsh training I received under the *Gunny's* tutelage. But there were lessons the old drunk Marine couldn't prepare me for. The McCutcheon demons had been passed down from one whiskey, blood-soaked generation to the next. Nowhere during bitter lineage did any of my Celtic forefathers ever break anything but the women that loved them and the jaw of anyone getting in their way.

My mother had suffered the family curse, as well as Amy, my older sister. The Gunny had a short fuse, and it seemed like no matter what the girl did, she made it shorter. Her hide always seemed to pay the price for it. Amy was strong though and never let the old jarhead know he hurt her. She would take her beatings, as they all did, in quiet supplication and tightened resolve. I'd wanted to step in every time the heavy hand came down on my big sister and even tried once. But a broken nose had made sure I would never be so ballsy again. I spent many nights crying into my sweat-filled pillow as Amy took her daily ration of 'discipline.' And prayed to God that he would spirit her away and save her from the old man's brutal hand.

My desperate prayers remained unanswered until twelve years later, when Amy decided to quiet the McCutcheon demons by swallowing the business end of a twelve gauge. The only thing the bitter Gunny had to offer at her wake was, *"The bitch had no honor… no pride. She was weak and only weaklings suck the bullet. Good riddance,"* the scathing liquor slathered words were wiped by the old man's sleeve and dripped from his poisonous lips.

That rotten apple didn't fall too far from that hell-spawned tree. As hard as I tried and fought, I was about to keep the chain moving down the line. As the rain-soaked highway before me passed by, my mind raced with memories both good and dark. I felt a tear build up in my tired eyes and knew damn well I needed that place to stop. On a gut hunch, I turned my right signal on and exited the highway in hopes of finding liquid salvation in a bottle.

Through the cold, rainy night, the half lit red and blue neon sign read: 'Moe Whiskey's Horseshoe Lounge and Bus Station - Best damn Bar-BQ this side of the Mississippi.' The sign glowed in the night and shone like a beacon of hope and deliverance. I didn't give a rat's ass what it meant. All I wanted…needed was a dry place to get a drink. Put this day behind me. Tomorrow was crawling toward me like a venomous spider, and I had no more control over it as I did the fucked up yellow tainted rainstorm pissing down on me. I was thirsty by all accounts, and Moe's would do me just fine.

The bar was a two-story, squat construct with a rickety looking awning off its right end, where a chugging silver Greyhound bus waited as a handful of weary travelers staggered from its open doors. About a dozen pick-up trucks and various other modes of transportation crowded the pothole-infested parking lot. There was even an old rusty John Deere tractor tucked between a blue Kenworth and puke yellow colored Chevy step-side. The rain was unrelenting and plastered the fading white paint from the side of the old building that looked two violations from becoming condemned.

I didn't give two-shits. They had cold beer, and if I was lucky, some nice Kentucky Bourbon. I pulled the 'Cuda next to a white Ford Pinto with fogged up windows. The back of the car bounced up and down hard enough to snap the shocks clean off. I just shook my head, parked, and got out. The temperature had dropped a good ten degrees. I straightened my collar on my brown jacket and pulled the tan Stetson over my eyes, heading for the bar door, while ignoring the lustful moans bursting from the rocking Pinto.

The heavy door opened with a mechanical mooing of a cow on my entry. "Oh, this is going to be just fan-fucking-tastic," I mumbled, and shuffled inside. The heat from the bar made me shiver as I surveyed the dimly lit barroom. The place was crowded and that sure as hell wasn't exactly what I was hoping for, but it would have to do. I'd seen my fair share of honky-tonks and hole-in-the walls, from Texas to Thailand. They all offered three things: booze, brawls, and broads. And I sure as hell had my share off all three as well. But tonight, I just wanted the drink. After the conversation went sideways with Inez before the flight from Washington, I couldn't get my head straight, so here I was, back on well tread ground. *Old habits die hard*, I thought as I approached the long oak bar to my left. Jamie Rogers crooned, *"In the Jailhouse Now,"* from an old jukebox way off to the right, next to the restroom and another exit. Again, old habits, but this was one that actually did do me some good.

The smoke-filled bar was packed with rowdy truckers and locals tying one on and looking to get laid. I was into half of that equation and tipped my hat at the brush-cut bartender. I noticed a few open tables beyond the dance floor, near the pool tables. I pulled out a Lark and lit it, as I found a table in the back near the pool tables packed with rowdy players. I sat down. I wanted to be as far away from the group of drunks dancing and carrying on. I took the jacket off, hung it on the chair next to me, exhaled the cigarette smoke, and kicked my feet on the opposite chair. The music was loud, and the place had far too many dark corners and blind spots, which made me damn nervous.

The Television above the bar had some reporter in New York City talking about some kind of disturbance, but hell, that happened every second up there, I thought.

Take a damn day off, ya dumb bastard, I told myself, and tapped ashes into the metal ashtray on the beer-stained table. The crowd was and half in the bag. I wanted nothing to do with them and was hoping to get the hell out of there after I got some chow and tried to call Inez again. It may not be worth two-shits, but I had to at least try. I snuffed the cig out and exhaled its smoky remains as a chunky waitress with huge boobs bursting through her Moe Whiskey's Horseshoe Lounge T-shirt approached me. Her peroxide blonde hair had seen too much treatment in her old years and looked like she had been rode hard and put away wet ten times over. Her blue jean shorts were tighter than she deserved, and her stomach seemed to desperately want out of their denim prison.

"Howdy there, handsome. What might I get for ya?"

She sounded tired, and I knew how she felt. I tilted my hat toward her and nodded. "Evenin'. I'll have a shot of whiskey and a Coors." I ordered not looking in the waitress's eyes. I filched a cigarette from my chest pocket and lit it.

"Sure. You be wanting some food, darlin'? I've got a menu." She smiled and held her hand on her wide hip.

"Uh, yeah. Just a burger and fries, Ma'am." I stood and inhaled the cigarette. I pulled a fifty from my wallet and dropped it on her tray. "Oh, and keep the booze coming, if you please."

"You got it, darlin'." She dropped her hand and turned on her well-worn heel, heading for the bar.

"Hold up." I leaned in and read her name tag, resting almost flat on her massive cleavage. "Uhm, Suzie, y'all got a pay phone?" I asked. My smile was weak.

"Right back there, other side of the jukebox, near the men's room, darlin'." She winked, and a smile creased her heavy made up face.

"Thanks." I tipped my Stetson, smiled, and walked past the group of drunken dancers and shouting rednecks stumbling around the red and blue light fake wooden dance floor. I was damn determined to take a day off, and it started right now. Five or six tough looking fellas surrounded the jukebox, laughing, and calling out letters and numbers of songs. I ignored the tough-guy looks they shot my way and saw the pay phone at the end of the red-lit hallway next to the shitters. I fished out a handful of change from my dungarees, picked up the receiver, and began shoving random coins into the slot.

I fingered the rotary dial for home, and the line crackled with static as it began to ring. I covered my other ear and leaned into the grungy wall filled with posted notes of lost dogs, old washing machine sales, and desperate souls looking for a blowjob in the cozy confines of the bathrooms not a nary five feet away. I chuckled as the phone rang and then rang some more.

"I Fall to Pieces," began clamoring over the speakers, and the entire bar hooted and hollered. I had to cup my ear and tried to hunch into the crook of the pay phone cabinet. The crowds seemed to know I was on the damn phone, because almost on cue, they raised their inebriated hoopla about a hundred decibels.

The line crackled and connected to home. As it began to ring, I hunched into the cabinet, hoping it would help me hear better. I counted twenty rings before the answering machine picked up. I found myself listening to my own cold voice. Damn. I do sound like an asshole.

"Hello, you have reached 213-212- 4395. Leave a message." It amazed me just how pathetic and miserable my voice sounded, even on a recording.

I felt stupid talking to my own voice, but I had to say something. "Inez, honey. It's me. I just wanted to talk to ya. Can you please pick up? I really want to talk. Pick up." I felt my heart sink as the machine clicked off.

No answer.

I slammed the receiver down and squeezed the hell out of it.

My gut wrenched, and it took all I had to fight back tears. I was getting goddamn tired of doing that. My hand absently touched my left breast pocket where the photo was. I chuckled at where I chose to put the last happy, visual memory we'd shared.

My heart began to pound as my mind replayed that day in the photo, and I felt warm tears roll down my cheek. The glowing moment didn't last long as the habitual pessimist took over in my head. *Hell, might as well be back in Washington for all the comfort it brought me now.* I was sure I mucked it up beyond repair this time. My face was burning, and I found my big fist clenching.

"Ya gonna ask that phone to dance or can I cut in?" A young girl's voice with what sounded to me like a New York accent startled me. Although, the faint smell of marijuana should have given her presence away. Damn, I was off my game. Not good.

I half-turned around, making sure the tears were all gone, and saw a teenage girl maybe sixteen or so standing there. Long black hair tied back in a ponytail. She had one eyebrow raised and an impatient look on her freckled face.

"Oh, uh yeah. I'm done. It's all yours, kid." I dabbed a tear that snuck free and tipped my hat before backing away from the phone, using my hat to cover my face.

"Thanks, Gramps. 'Preciate it." She snatched the receiver off the hook and turned her back to me. I noticed she had a backpack over her shoulders stuffed to the gills. A few candy bar wrappers peeked out from one of the pockets, as well as a Buck knife's handle. She talked tough, but I could tell she was tired. My guess was that she just got off the Greyhound bus. What was she doing traveling alone? It didn't sit right, but I remembered my promise to myself just seconds ago: *Take a day off now.* But I also noted there seemed to be bloodstains on both her jacket and backpack. I cursed myself and repeated, "A day off," as she searched her pockets, each time coming up empty. I reached into my pants front pocket, pulled out a dollar in quarters, and placed them on top of the dusty pay phone

"Thanks." She snatched the change up. She kept her back to me and stood facing the exit to the parking lot.

"Welcome," I said, giving the girl a tip of the hat with my forefinger and thumb. She didn't look, and it really didn't bother me. My concerns were miles away, and I needed a drink and some chow. I left the girl and headed back to my table and my drinks. I heard a jingle from the door beyond the pay phones from the parking lot. I stopped, then thought the hell with it, shook my head, and continued walking.

"A day off," I mumbled, and saw Suzie delivering my drinks. I suddenly knew it was indeed time for a day off. At least one night. I prayed I could salvage my marriage, but that would have to wait until tomorrow.

Still, something about the ballsy teen just didn't feel right. *Old habits die hard.* I grumbled, and took a shot, chasing it with the cold beer.

Buck Owens crooned, *"Act Naturally,"* when I reached my table to find the hamburger and fries waiting. I felt my stomach growl and sat down.

The food didn't last long, and I barely tasted it. I needed a liquid supper, but also knew far better to do that on an empty gut. Last time I did that, I ending up busting up a small bar in Nacogdoches, along with four bikers, my hand, and a couple ribs. This wasn't an option tonight. My world was already in the shitter and adding more crap to the pile wouldn't do me any good. I caught Suzie's eye and nodded her over.

"Y'all done, darlin'?" She chomped on her gum and smiled.

"Yes, Ma'am. I could use another Coors and whiskey if ya don't mind." I dabbed the corner of my mouth with the paper napkin and caught some commotion over by the jukebox. I leaned around the wide-hipped waitress and saw the rowdy bikers hooting and whistling as the young New York girl passed by, heading to the bar.

"Ah, pay no mind to those drunk fools. They're 'bout as harmless as a baby with boxing gloves, darlin'." She laughed with a snort and finished picking up the plates and dirty silverware.

"Be right back, handsome." She walked away and disappeared into the bright lights of the kitchen behind the dark bar. Half blinded from the contrasting white light from the kitchen and the cave like darkness of the bar, I gave my eyes a few seconds to adjust, and looked for the young girl and the assholes shouting vulgar offers and drunken promises.

The bar was heavy with cigarette smoke that created a wispy gray wall always moving and shifting through the packed crowd. After a few moments, I was able to locate the girl. She had squeezed between a short trucker with a beer belly and bushy, salt-n-pepper beard. On his head was a Kenworth ball cap, stained with grease and grime from miles of travel and road grunge. He smiled and nodded at the girl before going back to his dozen chicken wings. On the other side was a large woman squeezed into a pink Dolly Parton t-shirt. Her rolls of fat fought to escape the thin fabric and seemed to be winning. She paid no attention to the girl, caught my eye, and smiled. One gold tooth caught the reflection of the television above the bar. Her makeup piled on thick as a bar coaster. The women looked like a damn rodeo clown, and she blew a kiss my way. My disgusted inner thoughts must have shown up on my face, because she quickly followed it with a pudgy middle finger. I let out a small grin, but really wanted to ignore her, so I glanced back at the laughing bikers at the jukebox.

There were four of them. Two were big mothers with more ink on their bulging arms than in my entire comic book collection I had when I was a kid. The other two were a couple. A tall lanky dude with long blonde hair that hung down to his dirty blue jeaned ass. The other was a chunky chick with just as much ink and arm meat as the big guys. She was cat calling just as loud and dirty as the other shit-bags.

The drunken bikers were shoving each other and whistling at the young girl. She ignored them and dumped a handful of change on the bar. The light from the Pabst Blue Ribbon sign caught a glint of tears in her big brown eyes, as she talked with the old bartender. He shook his head, and she pleaded with him. He turned away, snatched a bag of potato chips from a stand on the back bar, and tossed them toward her. The action was so cold it even made my old, jaded soul flinch.

I was getting a bit annoyed and downed the shot, following it with a sip of the cold beer. My old instincts were rising. I knew I should let it go and just try to call Inez again. Although I knew it would end the same way the past five calls had. The same cold answering machine echoing my own voice, giving me the brutal answer I didn't, and couldn't, face or accept. Suzie returned and put a shot and beer on the worn wooden tabletop. My eyes never lost focus on the laughing bikers.

"Here ya go, sweetie. Need anything else?" She smiled and winked, one hand back on her jutted out hip.

"Yeah. Tell that prick of a bartender, that I'll cover whatever that girl in the green coat ordered." I leaned to look around the waitress. The girl snatched the small bag and shoved it into her backpack. She headed back toward the bus exit. The hooting bikers followed the girl out through the hallway to Bus Entrance.

"Shit...Never mind." I jumped up—kicking the chair backward—and followed down the dimly lit hallway.

9.

Arrested for Driving While Blind
Rt. 45 South
9:45 p.m.

The Caddy created a wide wake down the empty highway, spewing a yellow-colored wash behind it as it sped along into the Texas night. The strange haze was starting to freak Hector out as he drove through the torrential downpour. It wasn't just the fucked up colored rain that gnawed at his booze-filled gut, no, it was Isandro. He was different. His brother was a ruthless killer well before this last prison stint. There was something about his eyes. They were like dark caves. His shit wasn't wired tight and the way his brother was poppin' caps in civilians wasn't right. Not right at all. It was fucked up, and he didn't know what to do about it.

In the rearview mirror, he caught Isandro and his crew taking turns with the girls. Hector knew he was no angel, by any stretch. He'd stood side by side with his twin brother while they killed rival gang members and even gang banged bitches, but this was bordering on too much for even him. Hell, they'd just risked it all to break his ass out of prison, and now, he's killing and screwing anything that blows passed him, with no care in the fucking world. That kinda shit ain't right and is going to get them busted before they even get close to the Mexican border. He knew he should say something to his brother, but felt his tattooed chest tighten every time he considered it. He watched him and the others in the rearview mirror, and found himself confused. Half of him wanted to make the bitch, white-boy drive, so he could join in on all the partying, but the other half—the gnawing, guilt side—made his stomach turn. Sure, he loved nailing girls, but what Isandro was doing was bad shit, and far worse than he'd thought his brother would ever do. A screaming siren and red and blue flashing lights startled him from his dilemma, and he fought to keep the Caddy on the rain-soaked highway.

Hector watched as a Texas Highway Patrol cruiser flew by and quickly disappeared into the jet dark night.

After a few miles, flashing lights and bright red road flares split the night. As the Caddy drew closer, there were several Texas State Trooper cars and an overturned gas tanker, along with what looked like a Chevy Chevette. The car was much smaller and now crushed into the size of a grocery cart. One trooper stood in front of his cruiser. It's lights nearly blinded Hector as he shouted for the rest of drunk crew to shut the hell up.

Getting closer, the cop motioned for Hector to take the detour off the highway to his right. Hector let out a deep breath.

They made it through the accident scene, and now headed down a dark stretch of road that would still lead them to Mexico, it might just take them longer.

He knew he'd have to do something soon, but now wasn't the time. He flicked the rearview mirror away from his brother, and tried to focus on the slick road speeding toward him at one hundred miles an hour.

10.

Fool in the Rain
Moe Whiskey's Bar B-Que and Bus Depot.

I slammed open the door to the bus parking lot. What felt like a midwinter wind smacked me in the face. Stinging rain was its cold twin, and I had to shelter my eyes from its watery assault. I couldn't see the girl or the bikers, as the white wash of rain created a veil in the night, but could hear some laughter from off to the right—behind the idling bus in the parking circle. The yellow glow from the parking lot lights couldn't penetrate the pelting, driving rain. I followed the sound of commotion around the bus.

The hooting and hollering grew louder as I came up to a blue and white 1970's pickup and a black Olds Cutlass. The big bikers and their old ladies had the girl pinned up against the tailgate of the Chevy. The one biker had a cheap black tattoo of a cobra coiled around his left arm, and it was 'Cobra' who had the girl pinned against the tailgate while he sipped deep from his beer bottle. The other biker with long blonde hair stood behind him, patting him on the back as he laughed like a rabid hyena. The chubby biker chick held the girl's hair and was kissing her on the cheek. The whole lot of 'em were piss-drunk. It didn't change a damn thing in my mind and that was about to turn out bad for the rowdy bikers. The other couple stood behind them, laughing and cheering them on.

"Texas Ranger, on the ground, now!" I bellowed so they could hear me over the storm. I felt a smirk crease my wet face. The rain intensified and blurred the scene as they froze in place.

"Hooolleeeee sheeeeit. 'The fuck you be, hoss?" The muscle bound biker paused from licking the girl's ear and smiled at me. Their faces washed in yellow of the parking lot lights.

"See now, what we have here is a Texas Ranger. A hero." The big man let loose the girl's hair and stared straight at me; sizing me up. He finished off his beer and tossed it into the misty night. The breaking glass smashed the silence.

"Angie, don't let this tender bitch go. I've got plans for her. But first, looks like I need to take out some trash." The biker wiped his bearded mouth on his arm and walked slowly toward me. I didn't move a muscle.

"The way I see it, pig, is you're outnumbered here. Now, you gotta ask yourself, is this stray dog worth getting your dumb-ass head knocked in?" The big biker smiled with a broken grin that would have made a jack-o-lantern jealous. He started to flex his tattooed arms as he circled around me.

"That so?" I said, and slowly lowered my right hand to where my service revolver would normally have been. *Shit,* I thought, when my rain-soaked hand met nothing but more rain and wet jeans. I'd left the fucking pistol in the 'Cuda. And my back-up was in an ankle holster. No way in hell I was going to be able to reach it in time. "*I*mprovise, Adapt, and Overcome,"I bitched to no one and took a defensive stance, waiting for the drunken biker to make his move.

The oaf did. He shouldn't have.

The big man's swing was slow and sluggish. I easily sidestepped the clumsy blow, and then grabbed his arm, swept down to my side—cradling him against my waist. I took my left hand, placed it on his shoulder and pushed, while I twisted the lower part of the thug's arm away from his body. His shoulder made a wet, sucking sound as it popped out its socket. They big guy made a noise no man should ever make. He sounded like a six year old girl seeing a spider for the first time. I laughed at his pain as his slack body fell to the wet blacktop.

I lunged on top of the crying biker, driving my knee into the prone man's back. My hand swiftly found purchase on the handle of the Gerber Mark II knife, strapped to the inside of my boot, and I swept it around toward the rest of startled bikers.

"Let her go, and y'all can walk away." My words weren't an option. I knew if they went for me, I'd be screwed. But, this was the hand I was dealt and was used to not being lucky, so I hoped for the best. I held the blade in front of me and stared at the tall blonde, waiting for a response, good or bad.

"NOW!" I ordered, but somehow the impact was lost in the whipping wind and driving rain. The large woman stepped back and held her hands up. All the drunks did was glare through the fog as the girl ran behind me.

"Screw this shit. C'mon, Ross, let's get outta here," the tall guy said.

I eased off 'Ross' and let his buddy cautiously approach and help his now gimped up pal off the wet pavement. I stepped back. The drunk bikers knew this was a lose-lose situation and helped the big man with the broken arm to his feet. They shot sharp looks of *payback's a bitch* at me and disappeared into the cold, stormy night.

The cold rain painted the parking lot in a veil of mustard mist. I was damn grateful because there was no way in hell I was going to be able to arrest the scumbags, and the best course of action was to let them go. I counted myself damn lucky. The whiskey was on their side, and I knew too well I'd be on the losing end of that fracas.

"You okay, kid?" I slid the knife back in it's boot sheath, my eyes never left the retreating dirt-bags. I knew my words slightly slurred, but didn't really give a shit. I asked over my shoulder, not looking at the kid.

"Yeah...uh, yeah. I'm good," she said as I slowly turned toward her. The young girl's curly black hair was soaked with rain and smothered her head like a blanket. She took a breath and stepped back away from me, toward the awning of the bar. "Thanks. Thanks so much," the girl in the faded green Army jacket said.

"Good," I said as we moved underneath the rusty awning of the bus depot. I tipped my hat at the young girl and headed toward my car. I'd stopped too long as it was and needed to get the hell out of there.

"Wait."

The girl's panicked voice stopped me in my tracks. *Oh, hell.* I didn't need this shit. I'd done my good deed for the day, and the last thing I needed to do was to be driving around with an underage girl in the middle of the night.

I let some cold moments pass as I mulled over the options. There weren't many. I hated the thought of leaving her here, but dammit, she could be a whole load of trouble. I was starting to really dislike myself even more as I took in a deep breath of the foul air. The strange rain slapped the parking lot of the old bus stop. But...I stopped anyway.

Take a day off, asshole, I cursed and exhaled.

"Mister, where you headed?" she asked.

It sounded more like desperate pleading, and again, I felt my jaw flex and clench. I drew in another deep breath, scratched my forehead, and knew damn well I was going to regret whichever words came out my half-drunk, tired mouth. But yet, the words still came.

"Houston," I shouted over my shoulder. I kept thinking though, *Ah, shit.*

"Any chance I could catch a ride?" Her question came out tired, yet defiant.

"No," I said, as I walked away from the dryness of the awning. I didn't give two dead armadillo asses about the rain or the cold.

I was dead-ass tired, but after the shit-storm with the Governor, I didn't need any extra heat because of those biker scumbags. I needed to hit the road before this went any further south than it already had. The adrenaline was coursing through me, and I couldn't sleep if I tried. Staying here would be a bad thing, so getting home was a much smarter choice.

I should have known better.

"Ranger, I...I, have nowhere to go. No money an..." The teenager's voice fell to pieces, and I could hear her deep sobs through the drumming thunder and jolting lightning.

Day off, huh? I roughly rubbed my jaw and spun back toward the crying girl. *Fuck me.* I walked quickly to her, pulled a crinkled wad of cash from my wallet, and gave her a twenty. I adjusted my Stetson and turned away from the young girl.

"Stay safe," I said, pivoted on my booted heel, and headed toward my car.

"Please, I...I... Don't have anyone."

The girl's voice entered my ears like some twisted, guilt-ridden whisper. I imagined it would be how Bellia would sound if she were a teenage runaway. I stopped. I knew I was screwed. I couldn't leave her here—all alone.

Fuck me.

"Get in the car," I said as I opened the door to the 'Cuda.

11.

Old Man
Somewhere along Rt. 14

Cahill watched the rainy night fly by, and drank and smoked, but felt Mother Nature knocking on his back-door for over an hour. He saw an old abandoned rest stop that must have been there before the big Route 45 was built. He didn't care about all that shit. He needed to go. Hopefully, the place still had a toilet he could at least squat on. He hated dumping in the woods.

"Yo, bro. Ya gots to pull over, now." Cahill had to take a shit and could feel it getting dangerously close. The last thing he needed to add to the long list of things the Crew busted his balls about was him shitting himself. So far the quiet twin-brother of Isandro was a little bit nicer than the other. He heard Isandro's voice from the back seat, and it made him smile and relax.

"Yeah, pull over. I need to piss like a racehorse." The words from the leader made Cahill and his 'turtlehead- poking out' very, very happy. The car pulled off into the wooded rest stop. Cahill kicked the door open and ran to the small building that housed the restrooms. He skidded to a stop on the wet black top in front of a large padlocked wire gate. Looking closer, Cahill saw signs of renovation. *Cool*. He thought.

A hand-painted sign hanging from the fence, read the last three words he wanted to see:
'Closed for Renovation'
"Ah, shit." Cahill punched the sign and almost lost his load right there. He hopped and danced around, looking for plan B. He could hear the crew howling with laughter as he waddled

cautiously around the side of the building where he saw a dirt road. He hurried down the rotted leaf-covered dirt path to whatever shitting spot he could find.

The gangly kid was pinching his pale ass cheeks together as he searched for the best spot, far away from the watching, joking eyes of the brutal gang members. It was getting close, and he felt the 'turtle-head' poking out. He was seconds away from making brownies in his boxers. He found a fallen tree in a little canopy made by the leaves and pulled his jeans and boxers down. The tree truck provided a place to sit. Thanks went up to God as he finally took his dump.

"Damn, I got to stop eatin' Hector's bitch's burritos." Cahill grunted out a laugh and stopped quickly as he heard a loud hissing sound coming farther on down the dirt road. He finished and wiped his ass with big maple leaves, tossed them to the ground, and then noticed the deep tire ruts in the mud.

"What the hell?" he mumbled, stood and yanked his pants up, following the ruts. He walked into a clearing, and that's when he came upon a wrecked Lincoln Continental.

He slowly approached the car. It was impaled on a sturdy oak that would have needed another ten Lincolns to take the ancient tree down like a stack of marshmallows on a stick of maple. He paused, seeing the driver's side door wide open like a giant dove with a broken wing.

The storm raged, and the sporadic lightning flashes painted the trees in a wash of dark greens and grays, as Cahill bent down and cautiously peered into the dark shadows of the Lincoln. The rain pounded down on top the car like a thousand machine guns laying waste to the sheet metal roof. Cahill bent down to peer into the deep shadows of the car. What he saw made the burritos want to spew from his churning gut. Inside the smashed car, slumped over in the passenger seat, was an old woman, or what he assumed was a woman, whose entire face had been ripped and smashed into ribbons by the splintered windshield. Bright red blood mixed with huge chunks of broken white bone and shredded flesh. It reminded Cahill of the BBQ open-face sandwiches he loved. The sick thought made the contents of his stomach to hurl onto the side of the white car, covering it in chunks of reds, browns, and yellows.

The sight dropped Cahill to his knees as rain washed the puke from the car.

He struggled back to his feet and wiped the puke from his mouth on the sleeve of his red Adidas track suit. He leaned apprehensively back onto the car. The dead woman was the only person inside. The coppery smell of blood mixed with shit and piss, forcing him to reel away and paint the tire with the remainder of his stomach.

Three things happened to Cahill simultaneously. He heard impatient shouts from the crew back at the Caddy, the sudden realization that there wasn't any sign of the driver, and lastly, the feral snarl coming from behind him. He really wished he'd caught the last event first.

His scream was silenced by the pounding of thunder as an old man lunged and pinned Cahill against the side of the Lincoln. The man was surprisingly strong, and the clicker-clack of the old man's dentures filled Cahill's ears.

What the...? Panicked thoughts raced through the young kid's mind. The old man was trying to bite the gang-banger, and it took all he could do to stop the flailing bastard from taking a chunk out of his face.

Cahill felt his sneakers slip in the mud. They both splashed down into the rainy muck of the road as the old man's full weight forced him down. His heart felt like it was about to explode into a million meaty shreds, as he struggled to fend off the bigger man's attacks. The old fuck's gnashing teeth were mere inches away from Cahill's throat, and he cried out, but it was lost amongst the din of the raging storm.

"Get the fuck off me, yo." Cahill tried to shove the thrashing man off him, but the muddy soup of the dirt road fought against him. He found himself tiring against the old man's attack. He kicked his knee up into the attacker's stomach, but all it did was throw the old timer's biting mouth onto Cahill's neck. He screamed as he felt the fake teeth dig deep into his shoulder and tear a hunk of flesh free. He felt a searing pain fill him, and white flashes ruled his vision. He frantically reached out with his one free hand. It found purchase on a thick limb from the broken tree, and he gripped it tightly.

He shifted his hips enough to get out from under the old man; blood covered his face and bits of Cahill's flesh hung from his twisted face. Cahill rolled in the watery mud and held the large limb like a baseball bat as the old man stood to meet him.

"Motherfucker!" Cahill yelled into the cold, rain filled dark. White wisps gushed from his mouth as he ran toward his attacker. He froze in place for one split-second as he caught the old man's sullen gaze.

"What in he..." Cahill felt the words slip through his pursed lips. Black tears seemed to be pooling in the old timer's eyes and streaming down his blood-soaked cheeks. His mind was a blur with confusing images and sounds. The man lunged again. This time, Cahill jumped to the side and let the man fall face first into the door of the car, collapsing in a heap. The man sat, splashing around in the middle of a puddle filled with yellow rain-water.

Cahill raised the tree limb as the man tried to chomp at his legs. Cahill held the limb high as lightning flashed, bathing the clearing in white light. He lost his breath as the old man snatched Cahill by the legs. He fell clumsily on top of the old man. The thick end of the limb made a loud, squishing sound as it pierced the prone man's right eye, spitting blood into the rainy air. In one crazed motion, Cahill drove the wooden weapon deeper into the cranial cavity as he felt the man's eye pop.

He rolled off the old man and into the middle of the muddy road. It took few minutes for him to catch his breath and to try and wrap his drunk, stoned mind around what had just happened. He rubbed his eyes and squeezed his head, hoping it would wipe the nightmarish incident away.

It didn't work as he tried to stand up. His legs failed him, and he fell back down. He fought to catch his breath and stared at the dead man lying in the mud.

He heard the crew getting pissed and calling for him—threatening all kinds of grizzly torture if he didn't get his lily-white ass back to the Caddy. He stood, pain tore his shoulder, he touched it, and the bleeding seemed to have stopped. *Damn weird,* he thought. He looked from his wound down to the dead old man, who had the maple limb jutting out of his eye socket.

"Fuck this noise." The gang-banger shook his head and took some of the mud from his pants and covered up his blood-soaked hip. He pulled up the hood of his track suit, deciding it was best if he didn't give the assholes back at the car more reasons to bust his balls any more than they already do.

He turned, started back down the waterlogged road to the car, and a strange tingling began spreading out like lightning from the bite in his shoulder.

Once at the car, they asked him what the hell happened. He just shrugged and held back the wince of pain, saying he slid in the mud while taking a shit. They all laughed at him and climbed back into the Caddy, while he slowly got into the passenger seat.

The car pulled back onto the main road and sped off. To Cahill, the rain suddenly seemed colder, and the night, a bit darker.

12.

Riders on the Storm
Rt. 45 South

I was pissed. Pissed at the Governor. Pissed at the stupid rain. Mostly, pissed at myself. I never should have been suckered into giving the girl a ride. It smelled like bad news six ways from Sunday. I was damn sure I was already screwed. Adding this runaway to the mix was like ordering arsenic to my last meal of brisket and whiskey. But again, what do I do? Take a big fat helping and swallow it? Fuck me, when will I ever learn?

"Thanks for ...helping me back there," she said. I could tell she meant it, but the words came out like pulling a rusty nail from an old barn plank.

The last thing I needed or wanted to do was talk. I shot the long, curly black-haired girl in the worn green Army coat an annoyed look, hoping it would shut her up. I've never counted myself a lucky man. So far, this day was holding up its end of the shitty bargain, and this dark ride would obviously be no exception.

I said, "Welcome," and hoped the conversation was over. As usual, I was wrong.

"I'm Stacy Jo," she offered. She fetched a cigarette out of her backpack and then lit it. The blood splatters on the old bag caught my eye again. I filed it away and kept driving through the raging storm.

"No smoking in the car," I told her, and motioned toward the passenger side window. She mumbled something as she rolled the window down a crack and tossed the cigarette out into the stormy night. "Of *any* kind." I found myself letting a small grin go. She seemed like a smart kid—she'd catch my meaning.

"Sorry," Stacy Jo said.

He knew she caught him looking at her backpack or maybe smelled the herb, and quickly changed the conversation.

"You're a Ranger, huh?" she asked, tucking the backpack underneath her leg. She looked toward the ground.

"Yes'm," I said, noting her failed attempt to hide the pack.

"Sweet! You kicked the crap out of that shit-bag biker." She smiled.

"I'm used to dealing with those kinda folks," I said. I suddenly felt thirsty and groped my jacket pocket for the flask to only come up empty.

"I could have handled it, ya know." Her tone sounded defiant, and once again, a small smirk escaped.

"I'm sure you could have taken care of all four of them," I said and leaned toward the glove box. She slapped my hand away.

"Whoa, hold your horses, girl. I'm just fetchin' something out of the glove box." I held my hand up in a 'surrender' gesture and smiled at her. I was starting to like the girl's gumption.

She pulled her knees back and grabbed a hold of the backpack, as I opened the glove box and searched for the bottle. I shoved by back-up 38. snub nose under some paper work and kept feeling around. After almost driving off the slick, rain covered road, my hand finally found purchase on the cold glass. Once out, I slammed the door shut, opened the top with my teeth, and took a swig.

"Thirsty, Ranger?"

I could tell she was fishing for my name. Since any chance of a quiet ride to Houston was all shot to hell the minute I stupidly offered the girl a ride, I took another sip, and gave in.

"Yes, I am. Thanks for asking. The name is Jay McCutcheon." I wiped the excess whiskey on my sleeve.

"Glad to meet ya, Ranger Jay McCutcheon. Sorry about the flinching thing. It's been a strange trip from New York." She quickly turned her face to stare out the dark window as the last of her words flitted out like the raindrops that pelted it. I also noticed the strong grip she had on her backpack. I was pretty damn sure her gaze was fixed on something far darker and colder than the rainstorm beyond her window.

"Likewise. Where you headed?" I asked, sipping.

"Mexico," Stacy Jo stated flatly with determination, looking out the window.

"What's in Mexico?" I knew she was on the run. I'd seen the same look on dozens of kids over the years. They all shared the same distant, scared look—like they were running from some really bad shit, but they weren't too sure what kinda new shit they were heading to. This Stacy Jo was different. She had no fear hiding behind those bright blue eyes— no sir— just a lot of anger and resentment—a damn fitting attitude for the young runner from New York.

After a long thick, silence, she said, "Family."

The girl tugged at her jacket. I could tell she was trying to see where I was going with my clumsy interrogation.

"Ah, you have family back in the Big City?" I pursued, trying to keep sight of the yellow lines of the road. I didn't know why I was even asking, hell, I just wanted to get home. Maybe that was it; I was just trying to keep my mind off of what was waiting for me. Or even worse, what wasn't waiting.

"Nah, not really. Just a drunk dad who probably hasn't even notice I'm gone," she said in a voice that seemed to lose a bit of her swagger. Then she reached out for the bottle. I gave it to her, and she took a shot. "Oh, by the way, Ranger, not everybody who lives in New York lives in the Big Apple, ya know." Her ballsy tone and façade was back up and in place. I was damn sure there was more to this kid than she was showing.

"You tell me cowboy, where you bunkin' tonight?" she said with the worst southern accent I'd ever heard and followed with a forced chuckle.

"My road ends in Houston. I'm sure you can pick up a bus from there." I smiled and hoped that would put the idea into the young girl's head that's where the ride ended. "Oh, and you sure ain't gonna pass for no Texan, that's for certain." I grinned.

"Thank, God." She laughed, this time genuinely, and followed it quickly, "What's in Houston, Ranger?"

"My wife, well, fiancé, and daughter," I said before I knew it. The words slipped. I sipped again.

"Wow, congratulations. Was that who you were calling back there at the *redneck rodeo*?" she said with a smile.

I hated to agree with her, but being born and raised in Texas, and working in the Rangers, didn't do much to dispel the back-woods stereotype that most southerners had.

"Thanks. Yeah, but she didn't pick up." I could tell my words held more emotion than I planned. I could have, for the third time this day, kicked myself hard in the ass. I was really thirsty and really didn't want to explain my train-wreck of a life to a teenage runaway.

"I noticed. Everything okay, Ranger?" she asked and held her hand out for the bottle in my right hand. She smiled, and I handed her the bottle. She took it, sipped, and continued, "I'm sorry, it's none of my business. Ya just seemed pretty upset when you hung up the pay phone, is all." She shrugged and handed the bottle back.

I didn't know what to say. Here I was in the middle of the worst rainstorm I'd seen in years, probably lost my job, and to add piss icing to a shit cake. I was pretty damn certain that Inez and my daughter had already high-tailed it down to Mexico, and here I am wagging my tongue to some stray I'd just picked up in a shit-hole parking lot. Hell, the man upstairs has one twisted sense of humor.

"It's okay, kid. You ain't too far off," I found myself saying, staring into the wet night rushing by us.

"I just need to get home," I added, sipping from the bottle, I thought I'd change the conversation. "So, what you running from, and what's with the blood on you?"

13.

Woke Up With Wood
Rt. 14
Friday, 10:15 p.m.

The Caddy was running on fumes. Hector saw the red, white, and blue sign lights of '*ART's Gas-A-Torium and Truck Stop.*' He guided the big cruiser into an open pump. The rowdy Crew didn't even notice as he got out and began filling the car. The rain beat down on top of the huge gas station roof and reminded him of gunfire. Gunfire had become all too familiar for him. He'd been bangin' for almost ten years, and that was considered by most as close to godliness, or just damn lucky, Hector thought. He was tired, he'd killed, he'd raped women, beat the shit out of other gang members, and even civilians. But now, he was almost thirty, married with three kids, and just damn tired of the lifestyle. He'd only agreed to break Isandro out of prison because he was his brother. It's what his dead mother would have wanted. She never wanted them to get involved in the gangs. She had dreams of them becoming doctors, lawyers, and she even told Hector once that he could be *El Presidente* of the United States. It was something that made her glow with a smile wider than the Rio Grande.

Isandro wasn't the same brother he'd remembered. Gone was his loving, compassionate brother. Of course, he was a bad-ass with other gang members; you had to be to survive as the leader. But before he got busted, they'd get together away from the gang and drink and talk about their Mamma, and Papi. They'd share their dreams of quitting the damn gang and starting a restaurant in New York City, where their cousin Katie lived. They'd laugh, dream, drink, and talk shit until the morning light. All that was

53

gone after the botched hit on another gang's leader, where the man's entire family was slaughtered. Even the opposing gang leader's six kids. Hector believed in his tired heart that that's when his beloved brother Isandro died too.

The blaring horn of a white semi heading back onto the highway shattered his memory and brought him back to his dark reality.

He heard the click of the pumps shut-off and stared off into the storm raging all around him. He knew what Isandro was doing was wrong. He looked like his brother on the outside, no longer on the inside. Maybe he could talk some sense into him. Maybe the time in prison had changed him. Maybe God had answered Hector's prayers and had delivered Isandro back to him—the old Isandro, his blood. The brother he once knew and loved. He had to try, and something told him that the old brother was still inside the hard shell of the fully tattooed, angry man. The raping, brutalizing, and soulless killing was just his brother crying for help. If anyone could get through the thick, armor-like skin of Isandro Dianira, it was Hector. Once again his dreams were shattered as Isandro's cold voice ripped his prayers away.

"Hey esé, you gonna pump it or fuck it, yo?" Isandro said as he got out of the back seat, his hands and white wife-beater shirt, slathered in blood.

"What the hell?" Hector stepped away from his brother, staring at the blood. His head spun to the back window, and he peered through. As he feared, one of the twin girls lay limp on the back seat, like a rag doll that no longer had anyone to play with her anymore. Her throat lay splayed open, blood just beginning to coagulate from the fresh wound. Bobby held the dead girl's sister and kept her from screaming. Hector's mind raced—filled with images of the dead girl's eyes. All the eyes of the dead stared into him. Into his soul. Sweat raced down his face, and his heart pounded like a million jackhammers. Something had to be done. In a cold, sharp moment, he made up his mind. Then, solidified into one determined thought.

"This shit ends now, Isandro!" He stepped toward his brother; who was wearing a dangerous smile. Bone shuddering thunder rocked the gas station and yellow-tinted lightning cast dark shadows over his brother's harsh face. Hector jumped back as he could have sworn it was the contorted face of a demon. Bile rose in his throat, as his taller, stronger brother swiftly approached him— his grin now gone—replaced with a sinister sneer.

"What was that, brother?" Isandro's words hissed out as cold as the whipping rain all around them. Yet Hector could not, would not give up on his brother.

"You are better than this shit, Isandro. Mamma didn't raise us to be heartless killers and rapist. It's not too late, brother. We can hit the border and ditch these pendejos and leave this gang shit behind once and for all. Just like we used to dream about, remember?" Hector pleaded, standing up straighter now, with hands folded in a prayer gesture toward his brother.

Isandro tilted his sweat-covered head, and the smile returned to his angular face. His deep-set eyes squinted as he took his brother's new attitude in.

"Oh, so now my pussy-ass brother is going to save me from the fiery pit and make our dead mamma happy, is that it, esé?" Isandro spoke in a tone Hector had never heard before. It made his blood freeze. His heart ached with sorrow and fear. Hector backed out into the rainy storm as his brother slithered toward him. "Hell, holmes, you didn't seem to mind enjoying that fine pussy back there. What? Now you suddenly got some Jesus'er something?"

"No, that ain't it at all, Issie. I know you've been away a long time, but there's still a chance for you...for us." Hector never saw the fist coming, and white flashes of pain ruled his eyes. His head snapped back at his brother's ferocious attack. Hector collapsed into a puddle of mud as the storm raged all around them.

"This has been a long time coming, BROTHER. Let's get some shit straight." Isandro stood over Hector, and the harsh light from the gas station overhang cast Isandro in complete shadow. Hector felt his body tremble and his will seep into the muddy earth beneath him, as his towering brother continued his dark tirade. "I am the fucking El Presidente, NOT you, esé. You hear me? Do ya?" Isandro whipped a six-inch, bloodstained knife out of nowhere and held it to Hector's twitching throat. Isandro's white teeth splintered the black shadow of the gas station light.

"Brother, I...just wan—" Hector said. Trying to crawl backward.

Hector watched as something dark washed over his brother's face.

"Wanted to what, Brother? Tell me what *YOU* want *ME* to do? Stop me from having my fun? Is that it, *Brother*?" Isandro flicked his wrist, the blade of the big knife sliced into his brother's neck. Blood slowly dripped from the fresh wound as Isandro squatted down on top of his prone brother—his wide smile the only thing Hector could see.

Isandro was losing control, and Hector was getting worried.

"I'm the leader, brother. You follow me or I will gut you like a pig and eat your heart out and wash it down with tequila. You understand me, esé?"

Hector wept and nodded as the storm lit the sky, and darkened his soul.

"Get your sorry ass up and pay for the gas." Isandro licked the bloody blade and shot Hector a wink before hopping into the Caddy.

Hector's chest tightened, and a deep sorrow shrouded him. He wiped away cold tears as he walked toward the gas station.

A punch of thunder rattled the station and made Hector jump as he got to his feet. He hoped his shaking knees would hold up. It was too late for his brother. Tears escaped from his swollen eyes as he made his way to the Cadillac. He swallowed hard and was grateful now for the large trunk.

14.

Sure Got Cold When The Rain Fell
Rt.45 South
Friday, 10: 24 p.m.

I wasn't sure how to ask the kid, and had no damn clue how she'd react to my questions about the blood on her jacket and pack. I really didn't need the extra crap, but some habits just won't die. I could see her pull inside, not just her body, but her eyes and every part of her seemed to want to wash away in the damned rainstorm. I wasn't going to let her, *'Take a goddamn day off.'* The thought bounced around again inside my racing head. Some demons are hard to shake.

"I'm tryin' to help, kid. Honest. What's with the blood?" I tried to be subtle, but as usual, I was as subtle as a bull in a china shop. She looked at me with big blue eyes, over the collar of the all too familiar Marine Corps jacket, and searched for trust. I did my best.

"Kid, I am the Law, but inside this here car, you're safe as safe can be, so come clean," I tried again. The storm was kicking the car all over the road. The little red dummy light on the dash told me the gas was almost gone, but I wasn't giving up. Someone tried to hurt this kid, and something told me she had made damn sure whoever it was didn't win the day.

"It wasn't my fault," she spoke in a whisper—something I was damn sure this tough teenager from New York wasn't used to doing—I let her continue. She held her hand out for my bottle. I hesitated, but gave in. She took it and sipped deeply. Her big blue eyes never left me as I drove into the storm, looking for a gas station.

"What's not your fault?" I asked, taking the bottle back and jiggling it to make sure it wasn't empty.

"The fat guy on the bus...He ...tried to ra...rape me, that piece of shit," she vomited the words as if they were a confession mixed with proclamation. She turned her gaze out the dark window, but I could her see her fighting to hold back the sobs. She was a tough kid. Rock hard tough.

"Ah hell, girl." I didn't know what else to say. The more I knew, the more the lawman side of me would kick in. My gut told me this kid wasn't a cold hearted killer. I just let my words hang there in the stale air of the car.

After a long moment, she continued, "This guy had been watching me, since he got on the bus back in Pennsylvania, with his bulging eyes. I tried to ignore him, Ranger. I really did. He had perv written all over his dirty ass." She sat up straight. Her posture and tone changed into those of defensiveness. "The sicko kept looking at me and licking his fat lips like I was a Big Mac or something. Man, it freaked me out, so I went into the crappy bathroom, hoping to get away from him." She swallowed hard, and her breathing became short. She looked away as if to ignore the images running through her frazzled mind.

"He followed you in?" I knew the answer, but figured it might help her to get it out into words.

"Yeah." Her voice was small and distant, and I knew those images caught up with the poor kid.

"He busted in and I...I...told him to back off" Her cold wall was crumbling, and there wasn't a damn thing I could do. Hell, I couldn't even solve my own fucking problems. What made me think I could help her?

I searched my whiskey-hazed brain for a comforting response, but that was one of Inez's biggest bitches about me. Too distant...*disconnected,* the therapist told her. Disconnected my lily-white, Irish ass. You do my job for one day and you'd goddamn well understand why I wasn't always up for family 'show-n-tell' when I got home. Blood and guts weren't anything to me anymore. Senseless violence was like my first cup of coffee of the day—black, hot and steaming. Like a pile of cow shit—both are pretty damn plentiful in Texas—and just a fucking walk in the pasture for this Ranger. Hell, how do you come home, to your woman and your baby girl, and talk after leaving a crime scene where an out of work oil rig worker decided to string his wife and six kids up from their clothesline with barbed wire? Oh, and that was after he cut them all in half with a handsaw. He then had the balls to call and have us come down and kill his drunk, dumb ass.

Suicide by cop, my ass. I'd like to have strung that sick Motherfucker up by his balls and pick the meat from his selfish, sick bones. That's why I never talked much and spent my free weekends lost in a bottle of Jameson and repairing drywall. After all the shit that happened to me over the past few hours, this was the last thing I needed, but I still couldn't ignore the poor girl. I ain't that kinda cop or man. I sipped and continued to listen.

"I had no choice, Ranger. You believe me, don't ya?" She turned to me with a look asking for absolution. I sure as hell was no priest, but I did my best impersonation.

"Yeah, kid, I do." I meant it. I gave her a soft smile, as soft as my lined face could manage at least.

"You gonna turn me in?" She looked long and hard at me, her words came out in a cold, somber breath, and her eyes were wet in the corners. Her body was tense, and she clenched the backpack to her chest. I was torn between my job and my conscience.

"No." I gave her my word. I'd have to let it play out. Hell, my world could end tomorrow and all this shit wouldn't matter. It was then that I saw the hazy red, white, and blue fluorescent glow off to the right.

'ART'S Gas-A-Torium & Truck Stop.'

"Need to fill up," I said, grateful for the timing, and pulled off into the rain-slick parking lot, coming to a stop at an empty gas pump. I needed to try and reach Inez again, and Christ, it wasn't a conversation I wasn't looking forward to. It felt like my gut was fixing to boil over and burst out my body.

15.

Heard it on the X
Rt. 14
Near College Station.
Friday 10:37 p.m.

Cahill felt as though his body was about to burst on fire. The pain started in his shoulder, where that bat-shit crazy drunk old man tried to make a turkey sandwich out of him. Damn bastard almost succeeded too, if it wasn't for the young scrapper's lightning fast reflexes and ghetto-toughness. If only Isandro and the other pendejos could have seen him jam that branch through the old, but much bigger man's, eye socket. He was one hell of a bad ass and sure to be fully *made* into the gang once they crossed the border into Tijuana. He'd tried to take his mind off the searing pain shooting all the way down his arm and spreading into his sweat-covered chest. *This shit ain't right, yo*, he kept thinking while looking back at the Crew getting busy with the girl in the back seat. He knew damn well he best keep his dumb-ass mouth shut or it might be his head that gets kissed with the next bullet from the 'Boss's' gun. *Fuck that noise*, he added after each time he wanted to tell the Crew about his throbbing wound. In the end, he feared the Big Honcho, far more than any stupid infection. But still, he felt as though he was inside a freezer and his head was trapped inside a cooking microwave. Every part of his body stung with pain, and even his bones hurt like a bitch. There wasn't much the white boy could do but try and keep his swirling mind off the spreading agony. The only two options he had, were watching the bright and oddly mustard colored lightning strikes that seem to be racing the Cadillac, or the radio playing some kind of rock music Cahill's stepdad used to listen to. He thought the band was called,

ZZ Top, but after all the years, the pot, booze, and now the blinding shock of the bite on his festering shoulder, who the hell knew? He was almost asleep with his head resting peacefully against the cold glass of the passenger window, when the country rock tune was interrupted by a harsh, sharp blast of horns over the radio. A deep voice of a man followed, not the normal DJ, but someone sounding hot-damn important and nervous. Cahill leaned into the dashboard to hear better.

"We interrupt your normal broadcast with an Emergency Broadcast announcement."

The reporter's voice was controlled, but even through Cahill's buzzed and blood loss state, he could tell this wasn't no lame-ass hurricane warning. As the Crew in the back were hitting their peak, he had to lean in closer to the radio speaker to make out the dark words. He also saw that Isandro's brother, Hector, was wearing the same expression he was, and they both hunched to hear as the Emergency Broadcast continued.

"We have reports from the White House and the Pentagon that there have been what can only be explained as biological or nerve gas -type of attacks on all major cities across the country. The reports are coming in slow and sporadic, and I cannot speculate on the totality or the complete nature of the attacks in specifics, but what the C.D.C. and the Government is saying, is that as odd as it sounds, that anyone in direct contact or who is exposed to virus-like attacks, well, the survival rate is nearly 0%, and those who do succumb to the virus, seem to...rise from the dead and attack the living. A State of Emergency will be going into effect immediately, and all travel is prohibited. It also seems to be an airborne and is now spreading with the heavy winds that are coming off the Atlantic, spreading this virus toward the central and western part of the country. It is highly stressed by the White House and the Department of Defense that this is only in the best interest of all citizens of the United States. They ask that you please stay in your homes and do not leave for any reason and to please have patience while the C.D.C. and other agencies formulate a defense for these heinous attacks on our sovereign na..." Piercing static cut the man's last words off.

Cahill stared gaped mouthed at the radio and tried to wrap his head around what he'd just heard. He must be in shock, still drunk, baked or something. What the hell? He caught Hector shooting him the same, 'Oh, shit,' expression, but before he could speak, a stabbing pain in his shoulder and head took consciousness from him.

***

Isandro had been keeping one eye on the white-boy since the rest stop, and something wasn't right. He couldn't put his finger on it, but his shit wasn't right. He wasn't going to waste too much time on it though, after all, he had some fine 'Talent' that was performing for him and his Crew. He watched the twitchy kid in the Adidas jump suit with cautious interest.Smiling, he laid his head back and gently ran his hand through the girl's hair, continuing to force her to blow him. Knowing full well, he'd have to do something about the kid, and maybe, even his brother. He'd caught Hector eyeing him up and giving him 'questioning' looks ever since the blonde bitch back at the Mickey Dee's parking lot. Isandro didn't know what problem his twin brother had, but the puta had better get his shit wired tight or he'd be looking to hire a new driver fucking soon. The *Voice* kept whispering to him that Hector would be a problem, and that he should take care of it, before shit got bad. Isandro tried to silence the Voice, but knew deep down, he'd lose in the end and blood would be shed. He knew he should fight the dark desires, but like a drug, he needed, no, loved, the darkness, and even, the *Voice*.

"I'm getting' hungry, brother. I'm thinkin' I might need to feed my appetite soon, esé. Let's stop, got it?" He laughed as he finished and shoved the girl toward Hector. He watched his brother's nod through the rearview mirror, his eyes were jumpy, and sweat poured down his face. Isandro found a bottle of whiskey and chugged from it as he watched the two figures in the front seat of the Caddy, and wondered which one of them would try and fuck him over first. He sipped, smiled, and enjoyed the world he'd created, wondering how it was going to end.

16.

Every Night a New Surprise
ART'S Gas-A-Torium & Truck Stop
Rt. 45 South
Friday, 10:53 p.m.

I got out of the car without a word. The second I opened the door; the stench of rotten eggs, or maybe it was sulfur, punched me in the face. The air was heavy enough you could almost cut it like a thick-cut porterhouse. If I were a betting man, I'd wager this foul air wouldn't taste nearly as good.

"Whoa, what the hell is that?" Stacy Jo gagged as she got out on the other side of the car. "If this is what Texas smells like, man, I can't wait to get to Mexico, damn." She covered her mouth and nose with her jacket collar. "I have to hit the little girls' room, Cowboy, hopefully it will smell better in there." She managed to get me to crack a small grin as she headed toward the truck stop.

"It's probably just some shit whooped up from the desert and the Gulf. Bet ya, it caught a ride with this damn storm." I told her,not quite sure I believed it myself. Then realized I was talking to myself like a damn fool when I noticed that even the color of the driving rain had a screwed up yellow, mustard color to it. Odd, I thought, and took a sip from the bottle while watching the young girl walk toward the bathrooms; noting a '78 Pontiac Trans Am, a Dodge Little Red Express pick-up truck, and a Ford Econoline van with four men gathered around the open side door. They were covered in shadows and swaying like black balloons in a windstorm—probably drunk Mexicans coming up here for work.

I tucked the bottle back inside my jacket, pulled the nozzle from its cradle, opened the gas cap, and began filling the car. I watched the girl change her path away from the van and the drunk Mexicans. I chuckled. *They're just honest men looking for work girl*, I thought, and listened to the rhythmic clicking of the gas pump and the drumming of thunder waging war with the night above me. It was time to face the music and call Inez, to fill her in on my latest cluster-fuck. My stomach tightened, and I could feel moisture gathering around the corners of my eyes. How could I do this to her and baby Bellia again? How is one more broken promise and bullshit apology after another going to make her stay? Not this time? Goddammit Ranger, you really fucked things up beyond all recognition.

Click.

The harsh noise from the pump's automatic shut off slapped me upside the head and brought me out of my pity party. Make it right, McCutcheon, make it right once again. I tried hard to convince my old stubborn self that I could work such miracles, but something was telling me that this drunk, Marine, Texas Ranger, was running out of mojo and miracles. I screwed the gas cap back on and headed toward the station, rummaging through my pockets for some change to make the call. "Christ, figures. Can't I catch a fuckin' break?" I asked to no one but the pouring rain and flashes of lightning.

I was still cussing as the clunking and clanking of old bells rang when I entered the old gas station. The only person inside was an old man, whose gnarled body reminded me of a question mark. I'd take the over-under on if the old timer was working here when the Japs bombed Pearl Harbor. I nodded to him and tapped the brim of my hat. He just stared with a squinted face like someone was holding a bag of cow shit under his nose. I grinned and made my way to the coolers in the back of the store. I knew I was putting off making the call, but I wasn't ready to deal with Inez. For Christ's sake, how do I tell the woman that my stupid temper got me fired two weeks before our damn wedding? I stared at my reflection in the beer cooler and didn't like what I saw. I never did. I hadn't shaved or slept in a couple days. I was drunk and looked like death warmed over. What the hell was there to like? Then it happened; it began deep inside my gut with a burning heat that spread out to my chest and out to my arms and legs—a fever of anger that I could never control. It was a demon that had cost me one marriage, my Marine career, and now, odds are strong the love of my life and my sweet baby girl— Bellia. I leaned heavy onto the cold glass of the beer cooler, and it felt good. I needed to be cool. My breathing was shallow and harsh. It was an all too familiar occurrence, and I was damn tired of letting that sonuvabitch win.

"Say, boy, you okay back there or'n I gotta call the authorities?" The old-timer's voice matched his bent, weathered body. It forced a small crack of a smile in my taut face. I leaned away from the glass door and opened it. I took out a Pabst Blue Ribbon Tall Boy and turned toward the old man.

"Nah Sir, I'm right as rain. Couldn't decide just how to wet my whistle." I exhaled, holding the cold beer can to my forehead, and headed toward the check out.

"Well, son, this sure as hell ain't no museum. It's just booze fer cryin' in the sink." He rasped a chuckle and chomped on a cigar that was bigger than his crooked fingers.

"Yeah, that be certain," I said, cracked open the tallboy, took a sip, and then something green and fuzzy caught my eye off to my right. I placed the beer on the counter and squatted down in front of a display filled with stuffed animals. Instantly, my demon blew away like the cold, crap-smelling wind and rain outside. It made my heart warm as I picked up the plush, stuffed turtle with big, droopy eyes. Bellia was all I could see in my mind, and I heard myself say her name as I stood up.

"What's that, son?" The old-timer leaned over the counter.

"Bellia, that's my daughter's name. She loves turtles. That's what I call her." Those goddamn tears welled up again, and this time, I didn't give two golden shits. I knew now more than ever, that I had to make it work with Inez. I couldn't live without my girls.

"Ah, I see. Real pretty name." The old-timer took a puff on his cigar clinched between his yellow teeth and rang my beer up. "You gonna pay for that turtle, or ya gonna ask it to dance?" He reached out for the stuffed animal, and I caught a glimpse of the globe, and anchor tattoo on his forearm.

"It might be the best partner I had in a long time, old man," I said wearing a wide smile. He shot me a look, and after a long moment, smiled back, the smoking cigar still clinched between his teeth.

I added, "Semper Fi." My tone was serious, and he knew it. He paused, looked me up and down, nodded with understanding, and punched the keys on the cash register.

"That'll be $10.32, Marine." He coughed and took a sip from a glass with some brown colored liquid in it.

I handed him a twenty, grabbed the beer, and took a long pull. "Can you give me at least two dollars in change? I need to make a phone call," I asked, feeling like the old jarhead and I had a new understanding. Boy, was I wrong.

"'The hell I look like? A goddamn bank, fer fuck's sake?" He munched his cigar and blew the smoke out in swirling rings while making change. I didn't know what to say and sipped from the beer.

"Pelelue and Iwo Jima," he said and drank from his glass, winked at me, and I knew what the old man was saying.

"Tet and Hue," I said with a somber, knowing tone in my voice. The world had turned on its ass and here I was in a damn gas station in the middle of hell's half acre, having a Chesty fuckin' Puller moment with a crotchety old cashier. Damn strange.

"Oorah," he said, and pushed the change across the counter, holding his glass up in a soft salute. I returned it, and we both took a drink, both understanding that there are just some damn demons that no one can shake.

"Oorah." I nodded, and took the change, tucking the turtle under my arm. He pointed to the pay phone in front of the store and turned away. I walked out of the store, turned to the left, and wondered what the hell had just happened. My Mamma always said rainstorms always bring out the strange in the world, and I am thinking the old lady was spot on. I found the pay phone not far from the parked cars, set the turtle on top of the phone box along with the beer, shoved some dimes in it, and dialed home. The acid inside my gut grew with each static-filled ring.

***

Stacy Jo needed time to figure this out and to *light the fires*. What the hell was she thinking when she asked a damn Texas Ranger for a ride? She could feel her heartbeat in her temples. Hell, because she was a runaway or even worse, the baggie of weed she had stuffed in her backpack. He's probably calling his asshole buddies as she sat there on the crapper inside of this Texas rat-hole bathroom. She liked the dude. He seemed real enough, and he was pretty hot for an old man, but she was running on a short supply of trust lately. After the crap with *Fat Albert* back on the bus, she wasn't sure which way was up, and she hated that she wasn't in control. She fumbled through her backpack. Her stress-filled face spread into a wide smile as her hand found the over-stuffed baggie, and the very thought of its contents promised to take the stress away.

The storm pounded the thin tin roof above. The thunder rattled the stall as she fetched the doobie out of the case, put it to her lips, and lit it with her Bic lighter. The mildly skunky aroma helped to wash away the rotten egg smell of the rain. She hoped it would help her forget all about her current *Texas Ranger* problem. All she ever dreamed of was getting away from the Podunk town and her drunken ass dad, who'd rather use her for a punching bag than treat her like a daughter. And now, here she was, traveling with a cop, after gutting a pervert on a Greyhound bus. *How much more Twilight Zone could you freaking get?* she though,as she took a puff and held it in.

"Mom, what am I supposed to do?" she asked in a low squeak, as she let the smoke float out into the graffiti filled stall. She knew she wouldn't get an answer; she never did. She took another toke and tried to find comfort in the herb. That's when she heard the low moans and sounds of shuffling work boots on the wet floor of the bathroom. The pounding on the thin metal walls of her stall caused her to drop the Band-Aid box and joint. The thin door crashed open in an instant. She screamed and wished she were back in Arcadia Falls.

She screamed again, and the ballast of thunder silenced her.

***

Inez answered on the third ring, and the sound of her sultry voice and thick Mexican accent reminded me again why I loved the damned woman so much. Then, I remembered why I was calling her. The fire exploded in my chest again. My gut felt like I swallowed a dozen bouncy-betties that just went off. I felt sweat soaking through my dress shirt—even my sport coat—that was pretty damn odd, considering the damn temperature had dropped a good ten to fifteen degrees in the past half hour.

"Hola, Casa McCutcheon," she answered. Just hearing her happy voice made my hands slick with sweat. I almost dropped the damn receiver. I juggled it and finally caught it, and then put the cold plastic to my ear.

"Hey, baby. It's me," I said. I tried to keep my tone calm and cool, but knew damn well calm and cool were shot to hell the minute I slugged the Governor of Texas back in Lubbock.

"Hi, sweetie. I got your message, you okay?" she asked. "You sounded so upset," she followed up.

I took the beer off the top of the phone box and took a long swig.

The rain poured down, thunder rolled and sounded like John Bonham was playing a drum solo overhead.

"Yeah, Nezi. I'm good, well...not really," my voice broke, and my mind stalled. I didn't know how to tell her. My lovely fiancé wasn't a patient woman and never put up with my uncanny ability to beat around the goddamned bush.

"Jay, you never call me Nezi unless you have bad news. What the hell is going on?"

The damn woman knew me better than I did. No sir, there weren't no dancing around this conversation. I tightened the grip on the stuffed turtle atop of the phone box.

"Uh, yeah, you're right baby. I have some...bad news." I sipped from the tall boy again and watched the drunken Mexicans shuffling by the van, trying to get the balls up to finish my confession.

"Are you okay, baby?" I could hear the panic in her voice as it dropped to a desperate whisper. I'd heard it several times before. Usually it was when I was involved in a shootout and some kind of murder investigation. I was damn close to wishing I was shot instead of what really had happened. Hell, at least with a bullet wound I could heal. With this, I was pretty sure I would never recover from the shit-storm I'd run headlong into, like a stupid fool. There was a long pause before I answered. I could hear her shorten breathing on the other end and knew I needed to tell her.

"Nezi, I think I finally did it this time. There's a good chance I lost my job." There, I said it. It was out there in the thick, cold air, and out in the fucking open. As if to punctuate my bombshell, a round of thunder shook the building and the phone crackled with static.

A lifetime of silence filled the space between us as my heart began to tighten like vice-grips. And it felt like the sonuvabitch was getting tighter the longer that nothing came from the other end of the line. The fucking tears filled my eyes again, and I was going to run out of beer pretty damn quick. Finally, she broke the invisible wall between us and spoke.

"What? How…what?"

I could hear her shattered words, filled with disappointment and anger, burning like acid through the phone lines all the way from Houston.

I stared like a zombie at the men next to the van, not really seeing them. I was more like seeing through them—wishing I could be home. Be with my baby and explain things in person—but that wasn't going to happen. I started this and needed to finish it. My wet hands slipped on the slick plastic of the receiver. I drank from the beer, fought back the demons in my gut, and took a long, deep breath before I answered her.

"Hold on, baby. It's complicated…Let me explain…Please." I sipped again.

"James Mathew McCutcheon, what did you do THIS time?" Her words were full of venom and with justified indignation. I'd heard those same words too many times before to count, and every time they came out of her beautiful mouth, I felt as if chunks of my heart and soul were being cleaved with each and every goddamn syllable.

"Ya know how the Governor's been riding my ass like a rented mule since I got assigned to his goddamned detail last fall?" I started, and she cut me off.

"Don't take the Lord's name in vain, James," she corrected me as she usually did. It was one of the most annoying drawbacks in being in love with a devout Catholic. I tried hard to fight back my frustration at the damn cussing and continued.

"Right, right, sorry baby. Anyway, he started his shi- *crap* talking the second I got on the damn plane today. He kept asking to see pictures of you, and, ah hell, baby… worse." I couldn't bring myself to repeat what that bag of shit said about her. I felt my hand tighten around the beer can, so I took a sip to calm me down.

That's never is a good option for me. Damn demons.

"But, James. He's your boss. What did you do?" Her once sexy accent now turned into a deep, boiling tone of anger and frustration that if I wasn't careful, could probably burn my hick ass all the way from Houston. "Oh wait, let me guess… you lost your temper and slugged him, didn't you?"

By the ocean of silence I let pass, she damn well knew that's just what I did. My chest felt heavy and those fucking tears took up a perch in my damn eyes. I had to do something, but for Christ's sake, where do you go when you've been down this well paved road of good intentions that never ends in nothing but me fucking it all up?

"I know, Nezi. I know, but I had no choice! See, on the way back from D.C., he just pushed me too far." I knew the words came out hollow. The poor girl had heard those same words before, but it was all I had to offer. My flushed cheeks were quickly becoming soaked with tears. I wanted to punch something. "He was looking at your picture, baby, and sayin' really raunchy shit. I just couldn't…." The words came out like a rotted tooth painfully pulled piece-by-piece.

"Jay, you didn't…. You didn't hit him did…" Her word caught in her throat, and I could tell she was starting to cry.

"Sonuvabitch." I pulled the receiver away from my trembling mouth and leaned against the phone box, forcing my Stetson to teeter forward. I gripped the phone as if I could strangle the pain out of situation and make it all better. Who the hell was I kidding? I could never make anything better? Everything I fucking touched seemed to be cursed, like King Midas in fucking reverse. I drained the rest of the Pabst, threw it down on the rain soaked blacktop, and stomped it with my worn cowboy boot.

A long minute passed before I could form a word. The yellow tainted rain swirled and created a mustard-like haze over the parking lot. I searched for what to say next. I watched as the drunken Mexicans, who'd been singing and bouncing back and forth in this shit-full rainstorm, suddenly stopped at the same time. They all sniffed the chilly night air. Fucking weird.

Inez's voice shook me back to the heavy conversation. "Did you, Jay? Did you really hit the damn Governor? Please tell me it's just one big joke…. Please!"

I could tell she already knew the answer. My heart felt like it was going to shatter into a million pieces and wash away in the storm. I kept an eye on the drunks, but every other part of me was with Inez—in Houston. And wishing I could make it better. Wishing I could lie and tell her no, I didn't hit that fat sack of dog shit. But on some level, I didn't regret knocking the old fuck on his perverted ass. He deserved it, and I should have done it months ago. On another level, a far more important level, I knew I had just driven the last nail into my own pine box. There sure as hell wasn't going to be enough, heartfelt apologies,,or enough roses, or promises of, 'I'll change and I swear I'll never do it again.' I'd worn them all out like the worn whiskey flask inside my jacket. I was pretty damn sure I was a day late and a fucking dollar short on this one. And her words confirmed my worst fears.

"He's an old drunk, James. How could you punch the Governor of Texas? Have you gone loco?" she asked.

The drunken Mexicans slowly moved toward the building. I kept watching them. I didn't know why.

"But, Nezi. The things he said…they were so na—" She wasn't having any of my lame-ass excuses.

"Drop the *Nezi* shit, James. We've been through this before. San Antonio, Nacogdoches and New Orleans and now THIS!"

Her words made my breath freeze in my chest. She, as usual, spoke the gospel, but it tore at me like the hellhounds I'd been dodging since 'Nam. I was sure we both remembered the horrible memories of each incident and what happened because of them.

"You promised me you were done with the fighting and the drinking." A short pause filled the chilly air with razor-sharp anticipation.

The drunk Mexicans reached the bathroom doors of the truck stop. A close lightning strike lit up the rain slick parking lot and I shade my eyes.

"I tried, baby. I really did. That asshole, just pushed me too…" She didn't give me a chance to finish.

"James…I'm done. I love you, but I just can't…. I can't. Not anymore. I am too tired, and I have to think about Bellia now."

She was balling, and I felt as though those fucking hellhounds were ripping the meat from my bones. Deep down, I knew I deserved it. It didn't take the pain away, hell no! It was right there, front and goddamn center. My tears matched the fucked up storm raging all around the godforsaking truck stop.

"No, baby, don't. Please!" My words came out weak and pitiful. I was damn sure there wasn't a fucking thing I could say, no promise I could swear to her, that would make her change her mind. After all, why should she? I was a lost cause. I was a drunk who liked to fight, and as she always told me, I was born a hundred years too late. I should have been riding with Wyatt Earp and Doc Holiday, drinking whiskey and meting out my own brand of whiskey-juiced, cowboy justice. Hell, maybe she was right. I had more demons trailing me than I had bullets to shoot them with. I was damaged from the damn get-go. I was sorry.

"I'm sorry, James. I love you…but our daughter needs to be safe and I don't know if I can tru…. I can't keep this up anymore. I am sorry, James. I…" She hesitated.

She didn't have to finish. I knew what she meant, and it tore at me; the truth always does—bores deep into your flesh like a fisherman's hook. The sharp metal never stopped for anything. The truth was the truth. Inez was right.

"Wait, Inez… please. This time, it was really different. Skip will tell ya." I had to try. There was a pause in the storm, and I saw the drunk Mexicans disappear into the bathroom. The women's bathroom, and a shrill scream broke through the rain.

The kid... I panicked.

"What in heaven could he possibly tell me that I haven't heard a million times already, James? Really? I love you, and I don't want to go. You know I love you so much, but what can you tell me, to make me stay?" She meant her words. She never talked bullshit.

Screams came again from the bathroom. I never could take a day off.

"I know, Nezi, but please just trust me. Baby, I gotta go." I dropped the receiver and sprinted through the mustard colored rainstorm, praying I wasn't too late.

"James? James? You there?" came through the swinging pay phone receiver as I ran. My heart trembled, and my tears matched the falling rain, but the New York kid was into something bad. I can never take a damn day off.

Fucking demons!

17.

Rough Boy
ART's Gas-A-Torium's Restroom
Friday, 10:59 p.m.

Stacy Jo found herself backed into the slimy corner of the bathroom stall. Her feet slipped on top of the crap and urine-stained toilet—frantically flailing her knife at the four men, who crammed into the small stall like a feeding frenzy of sharks who could smell blood inside the diver's cage. She could hear herself screaming.

The men were shouting, no, groaning at her. She had no idea of what they were trying to say.

The smell was far worse than the rotten egg odor outside. This new stench choked her, causing her to gag, and it reminded her of two-week-old road kill. Stacy Jo fought the bile back down into her throat as she swept the knife at anything that grabbed for her. She felt the blade slice deep into the forearm of one of the drunks, but the guy didn't react at all, the bastard just kept coming at her, trying to grab her. They all had the same mad look in their eyes. Their eyes were black, yet sad looking, and in the chaos of fighting them off, she could have sworn she saw black tears streaming down the dirty men's faces.

"Get the hell away from me you mother —" The words were hers, but she felt like she was watching a scene from a cheesy horror flick—distant and detached. They snarled and bit at her, trying to pull her closer. *They want to eat me,* that sudden, sick thought snapped in her mind. Her blood ran cold as one of the attacker's rotting teeth chomped in the air, inches from her face. She swung the blade across one of the attacker's cheeks. Renting his flesh loose from his face, but no blood came with it. She pressed her body against the cool wall, and kicked and stabbed at them. She was getting tired, and her lungs burned from yelling for help. One of the other men wearing a *Loverboy* t-shirt, grabbed her arm, yanking the knife from her hand. It clanked onto the wet, tiled floor. She punched at the man's tattooed arm. He hissed at her and pulled her closer to his wide-open mouth. She cried out and continued to punch and kick, but the man was too strong. She felt a sharp pain tear through her sneakered foot as one of the other men bit down into it. She screamed and jammed her thumb into the man's eye socket. It made a sickly, squishing sound as she buried her thumb knuckle-deep. She then felt her other foot slip on the sweating plumbing of the shitter. She fell onto the cold, wet floor and knew she was dead.

A bright muzzle flash filled the small stall. One of the attackers fell away and another was yanked backward as a booming, commanding voice followed.

"Down on the floor," she heard the Ranger shout, as the other attackers turned away from her and lunged toward the sound of his voice.

She grabbed at her foot and looked for blood, and then watched the Ranger move smoothly, seamlessly, as he took on the men who were grasping and biting at him. Biting...why were they trying to bite? Drugs? What the hell? She puzzled as she watched the drunk Ranger take one man by the wrist and jerk it down. The growling man fell to the floor.

The Ranger followed his attack with a smash to the back of the man's skull with the butt of his .45 pistol. Spinning underneath another one of the staggering men, he kicked out with one of his cowboy boots and hit the man on the side of his knee, causing him to topple on top of the other attacker and they both landed in a heap on the wet bathroom floor.

"Go!" He glared at her as he brought a fist against the prone man's temple. He jammed his broad body between her and the attackers.

She knew this was her chance. She heard gunshots as she scrambled out of the bathroom into the raging storm.

She looked back as she got to her feet, for a sign of the Ranger. Nothing. Once back at the Ranger's car, her head swirled with the insane uncertainty of questions, ideas, and crazy images of men trying to bite—no—eat her! She whipped the door open. The yellow glow of the dome light was lost in the mustard colored haze of the storm and rain. She collapsed inside the car, stared back at the bathroom, and hoped...prayed.

***

What the hell was wrong with these guys? No response when I told them to stop and drop. All they did was turn and came at me like goddamn nut-jobs. Junkies, must have been on PCP, or something. Not like I had a lot of time to do a blood test or ask for fucking I.D. They looked at me with tears in their damn eyes and all the while trying to bite me. What the hell was going on? No time to ask...just react. I had no choice but to pull one them toward, away from the girl.

I told the kid to run as one of the druggies grabbed me from behind. I heard his teeth snap the air, too close to the back of my neck. I tucked my opposite shoulder underneath me and rolled, it wasn't graceful, but it worked. It brought the attacker with me which allowed me to get my right leg up high enough that I could smash it down on his nose with enough force to crush cartilage and bone. I heard the snap and smiled. As I stood I wobbled a bit, but found solid footing, just in time to see the last drunk shit-bag try to bite down on my arm.

The force of his attack sent my pistol crashing to the floor, but I spun away from the bite just as it caught my sleeve. The man's weight sent me to my knee, but that was okay. My hand jutted out and found purchase on the knife strapped to the inside of my boot. I swung it up, and in one direct motion, buried it deep into the man's eye socket. He immediately dropped and collapsed in a heap on top of the other men lying on the floor of Whitney's Gas-A-Torium.

I stood there wondering what the hell had just happened? Four men; all with the same goal; to bite the kid and me. Their eyes soaked with black tears. What in the world was going on here?

And the smell…. They smelled like ripe bodies we'd pulled out of dumpsters or riverbanks. The bastards didn't even flinch when I shot or cut them.

They all lay at my feet. The stench of death all around them, but I had spent the better part of the past hour watching them back at the van, and now this. Christ, I needed a damn drink. I didn't know if I should call it in or just let the shit go. I was pretty damn sure I was out of a job the second the sun came up, so why bother?

I kicked one of the bodies to the side, picked up the knife, found my gun, holstered it, and walked out.

This shit ain't right, I thought, and something told me I just screwed myself way beyond my pay grade. I walked back out into the pounding storm and saw the kid waiting inside my car.

"Okay, now what?" I asked to the dark, crying black sky.

I walked to the pay phone and saw the turtle lying lazily atop the phone box with its head tilted off to the side, staring at me, with its wide, sad eyes. "Go to hell, Leonardo." I snatched the toy from its pious-perch and caught the sight of the phone's receiver swinging wildly in the storm's cold wind.

"Fuck me running." I quickly grabbed it and prayed that she'd still be there.

"Goddammit." I felt my shoulders drop and thought, that once again, the Man Upstairs had better things to do than listen to my dumb ass. I hung up the phone and ran back to my car. I knew the right thing to do was to call the crazy shit into the local PD, but my head was a scrambled mess. Half drunk and couldn't think straight. I lost my job, lost my wife and baby, and now, I have a runaway from New York riding with me. A runaway who I just saved from a bunch of freaked out, black tear-crying druggies. Hell, if you add this almost Biblical storm kicking Texas' ass, you might think that it's the goddamn apocalypse. A dark chuckle came from deep inside my gut as I opened the car door, tossed the turtle onto the backseat, and got in.

"The hell with it. If the world's going to end, I'm at least going to see my woman and baby girl," I mumbled, and shot the kid —shivering from shock, I guessed—a look, and closed the door behind me.

"Fucked up night, huh kid?" I stated, knowing the answer and started the engine, and pulled out back onto the highway. Houston was roughly fifty miles away, and I couldn't get the hell away from this cluster-fuck soon enough.

The odd thing was, and I sure as hell hoped I was just seeing things, but I could've sworn that I saw something through my rearview mirror that sent ice daggers up and down my spine—those drugged up Mexicans staggering out of the shadows of bathroom back at the gas station. I shook my head and tried to focus on the slick road ahead of me.

"No way," I told myself, and fished around my jacket for my bottle. I muttered to myself, "Out of the damn frying pan into Satan's asshole," and tromped on the gas pedal, heading west.

18.

Thank You
Rt. 45 South
Friday, 11:30 p.m.

I drove in silence, and the girl just leaned against the side window, staring out into the swirling storm. I was pretty messed up and was damn sure she wasn't thinking too clearly either. The Allman Brothers kept playing over and over on the tape deck, and every time one side finished, it would click, flip, and play the other side. I wasn't listening and couldn't give a rat's ass. I had too many voices in my head, all vying for attention, and my head felt like scrambled eggs mixed with razor blades inside a damn blender.

"You okay?" I asked as the girl took her tennis shoe and sock off, roughly checking out her foot. I could hear her breathing—jagged and raspy. She was scared blind.

It took her a few minutes of scouring every inch of skin on her small foot. She sagged back into the seat and let out a big breath of air.

"Yes! Damn. What the hell was that back there, Ranger?" Stacy Jo finally blurted out, nearly causing me to crash the damn car. "Those nut-jobs tried to freaking bite me."

"I've got to run to keep from hidin'," The Allman Brothers sang, creating a buffer for me, because I had no damn clue as to what those men were all about. I searched and searched inside all my years in the Corps, years as a Ranger, but all I kept coming to was diddly squat. Inez and Bellia's faces kept racing in front of

79

any rational explanation I could think of. I couldn't even try to wrap my head around that shit.

"Drugs," I heard myself blurt out, in a tone that sounded like I was trying to convince myself a whole hell of a lot more than the wide-eyed girl in my passenger seat.

"Cross roads, will you ever let him go? Will you hide the dead man's ghost?" the haunting song played on as the yellow tainted rain pasted the windshield. The wipers had all they could do to keep the damn glass clear. Odd shit, all around.

"Drugs? Really? Those crazy assholes were trying to fuckin' bite me like I was a damn Snickers bar, man?" The kid screamed and made a chomping motion with her fingers. "Ya know, like Jaws?" She added, jutting her hands out at me, miming a damn shark attack in my face.

"Yeah, yeah, for Christ's sake. I get it." I smacked her hands way and shot her a look, as I adjusted my hat and tried to keep the car on the road. "You're welcome," I added, giving her a quick glare.

"Hey, don't get me wrong, I appreciate you riding in like the Lone Ranger and all, I…I just never seen anything like that before. I've had my share of my Dad's drunk-ass pal's trying to get their groove on with me, but at least with those dirt-bags, I could always punch 'em in the sack and they'd high-tail it. Those dudes back there were…were…." She slumped back into the seat and didn't finish her thought.

"I know," was all I could say. I kept trying to shake the images of the forms shambling out the bathroom. It made no sense at all. I jammed a knife into one of their eye sockets and either cut or shot the others. Nobody gets up from that kind of damage. Not from my experience, at least. But the way this godforsaken day had been going, who the hell knows what could be going on? Every time I tried to focus on the bathroom thing, thoughts of home crept back in. I fought like hell to keep my tears out of sight of the kid.

"I cut one of 'em, and the guy just kept snapping his damn teeth at me like he hadn't eaten in a damn month. What kind crap is that?" Her head whirled around, as if looking for an answer inside the car.

"I did too, kid. I even had to shoot them." The word flew out before I knew it and really, didn't care. A day late and a damn dollar short to be worried about police protocol at this point, I told myself.

"One way out baby, I just can't go out that door." The Allmans kept playing and I could see the girl getting annoyed. I liked the music. It helped me avoid conversations. Like this one where I had no solid base to start from or any sense of goddamn center. Inez was leaving me, druggies were having the worst case of the munchies I'd ever seen, and I have to try and explain all this shit to a seventeen year old girl. What the hell did I do in a past life to deserve this kind of shit-filled karma? I reached over to turn the volume up on the radio. She slapped my hand away and roughly punched the cassette out of the player. I could feel her hot stare; looking to me for answers to the trainload of shit that had just happened.

"What the hell are yo —" The radio blared with an emergency alert and cut me to the quick. I glared at the green glow of light from the radio. My gut tightened and told me things were about to get a hell of a lot more Twilight Zone-esque. The words that came next from the radio alert proved me far more spot on that I damn well wanted.

"This is an Alert from the United States Emergency Broadcast System and this is NOT a Drill. We repeat. This is NOT a drill. Due to several terrorist attacks on several major cities in the United States that have released what the CDC can determine at this early stage as nerve agents, the Governor has called for no unnecessary travel. So if you are on the road, you must find shelter immediately. Do NOT; I repeat NOT try and search for loved ones or family members. Go to the nearest Emergency Shelter and seek refuge there. Stay tuned for updates." Then the radio cut out and the speakers filled the car with harsh static.

I pulled the car over onto the shoulder of the highway and slammed it into park. We sat in empty silence as the words from the radio alert and the bizarre events of the past hour mixed together in my head like a jumbo cocktail from hell. I looked at Stacy Jo, and her look must have mirrored mine, because I was feeling as shocked and confused as the look on her young face.

"What the…" was all I could utter as thunder shook the car and spastic lightning flashes created harsh, demonic shadows all around us. We were just in the middle of east-Jesus, where the hell were we supposed to go? Just when I thought this weird storm couldn't get worse, the wind picked up and was pushing the car around like a goddamned Matchbox toy. The rain fired down like cold bullets from the black night sky.

"What are we gonna do?" Stacy Jo's words came out in a meek whisper; sounding more like a little girl than a seventeen year old. The sound reminded me of my Bellia, and those goddamn tears crept back into my eyes. The thought of Inez and her alone shattered my damn heart. I swallowed hard and forced myself to focus on the task at hand.

"There was only one place that's close enough, that I know of," I said, fighting off the demons deep in my gut, and looking out into the rain-wracked night—which was only broken up by violent flashes of bright lightning and my own tortured imagination.

"Where?" she uttered.

I didn't answer her. I just put the car into gear and drove west… Toward Houston.

After a few miles, over the rise, the tell-tale lights of emergency and police vehicles lit up the night sky. I slowed the Cuda down and crested the ridge to see a gas tanker, tits-up, and a not-so-lucky compact car even more compact. I knew some folks were dead, and this wasn't good. There was a *Statie* directing traffic at the fork in the road, and while I would normally stop and see if I could help out, tonight was not the night for brotherly love. I waved at the guy and turned onto old Route 14. I didn't like that this little detour would add miles and time to my drive, but the way the day was going, I wasn't going to bitch. It seemed I'd already pissed off enough gods for the day.

19.

Life's a Misery
Jimbo's Rusty Cactus Diner & Blue Sky Drive-In
Rt. 14
Friday, 11:34 p.m.

"Jesus H. Christ, where the hell is Ellen? Robbie Casella bellowed toward the kitchen of the roadside diner, her half smoked Lark clinging precariously from her full bottom lip. She glimpsed up at the Elvis Presley clock hanging on the yellowing wall and shook her head. "Oh, wait, don't tell me, Jimbo, *'My goddamn car won't start and that low-rent man o' mine is off drinking down at Finn's again. Or, I'm sorry Jimbo, but this storm is really, really bad and ya know how bad my eyesight can be,'* did I get that about right?" She smiled, her wide face still held the beauty of her fifty-five plus years on the planet.

"Well lookie who wins the prize at the bottom of the Cracker Jack box." Jimbo poked his stubble-covered, round face through the serving window that separated the kitchen from the counter. His thick white muttonchops hugged his rosy cheeks and huge, yellow-toothed smile. He smacked the bell on the counter with the flat of his spatula and shot Robbie his friendliest grin. She knew all too well what the next words were going to be, regardless of how high he piled the sugar on.

"Oh, ain't no way in hell, I'm takin' her shift *again*, Jimbo!" She placed the plate of biscuits and gravy down on the worn counter in front of a lanky trucker who reminded Robbie of one of those hippie ZZ Top boys she'd seen on TV.

83

"Can I have some more coffee?" The Trucker's words fell on deaf ears as Robbie spun on her well-worn heel, one hand on her wide hip, and squinted back at the portly diner owner.

"You do realize I just worked a ten hour shift at this hell-hole, right?" she said through pursed lips and adjusted her peroxide blonde hairdo, waiting impatiently for a response.

"Yeah, Robbie, I know, but what do ya want me to do, huh? Ellen's about as reliable as a damn Pinto, but I can't do this myself. And hell, the storm out there is ragin' like a goddamn bitch in heat. I got a feelin' that we'll be seein' a rush of truckers and other poor folks out there needin' a place to ride the storm out, so what you say, Robbie?" Jimbo's head popped back through the service window, with his hairy, thick arms held out in an exhausted shrug. "C'mon, honey. Look, I'll make it well worth your while." He gave her a long, promising wink, and his bushy white eyebrows played along with the accompanying teasing grin across his unshaven face.

The storm pounded the small diner, and the yellowish colored rain pelted the windows. Robbie knew that, once again, she was going to get screwed, and not in a good way. She buckled and adjusted the horn-rimmed glasses on her face, letting a small smile break across her lined face.

"Oh, like that's going to be a real deal breaker." She let out a dull chortle and waved him away back into the kitchen. "Yeah, yeah, whatever, buster. *'Worth my while,'* is a damn raise, and I ain't seen one of those since Carter was President. So, just keep your winkin' to yourself, mister." She snuffed out the cigarette in the metal ashtray next to the cash register, still shaking her well-coiffed hairdo.

"Okay, Okay. How's about the next two weekends off, and to put the cherry on top, good lady, I'll even let you take me out to the drive-in to see the new Police Academy flick? What do you say, hot stuff?" he held the spatula to his grease-stained, once-white shirt, and tilted his head and smiled. His bushy eyebrows promising a very romantic evening.

"You own the damn drive-in, ya cheap bastard." She fetched another cigarette, lit it, and waved in an irritated motion at the young couple in the booth by the bathrooms, who seemed to want something.

"Weeeellll?" Jimbo's eyebrows weren't taking no for an answer, and although her damn legs felt like they were swollen to the size of the goddamn Goodyear blimp and her damn corns were about to catch fire, she gave in. She always gave in. "Asshole"she cursed the burly cook and flipped him the bird, took a drag from the cigarette, and limped over to the two lovebirds holding hands and making kissie-faces. If the fat man in the kitchen didn't make her want to puke, these kids were a close second.

"Yeah, yeah, your broke ass better buy the popcorn and bring the Southern Comfort," she bitched, and not one ash ever hit the yellowing black and white tiled floor of the grungy diner.

The trucker was still holding out his empty coffee mug as she walked away. Lightning washed the old eatery in a yellow wave, and the storm obscured the slow, slumbering forms making their way down the hill from the Leonard County Cemetery.

20.

Lowdown in the Street
Old Redeemer Cemetery
Rt. 14
Friday, 11:47 p.m.

In life, Carol Highshoe was a writer—a storyteller of all things glittering with gold and silver—all things fantastic and otherworldly. She had dreams of becoming the next Marion Zimmer-Bradley or Jackie Gamber; telling stories of powerful women and beautiful dragons. But a week ago, while she was sitting at her writing desk, cup of tea in hand as she was about to type 'The End' on her first novel, fate decided to throw this poor young woman a deadly curveball and let loose a blood clot that raced to her heart, ending what could have been a stellar career and an amazing life.

In death, moments ago, her eyes popped open. She began to dig and crawl upward. Her nails burrowing, pulling the rain soaked earth away as a newfound hunger filled her. An overwhelming urge poured through her embalmed body, causing it to push on in pursuit of her new goal.

Once on the surface, rain pelted her pallid skin. She felt two distinct urges filling her: one was to feed. She could feel heartbeats in her undead mind, this made her sewn mouth drool, or at least want to. The other vague urge was to turn northward and walk. But the overwhelming hunger ruled. She could sense food was close, and as she rose to her feet soled in high heels, which she hated, she realized her mother must have had her buried with them. That bitch would have known she hated to be stuck eternally in a mauve

86

dress and high heels. She cursed and followed the urge as she staggered awkwardly down the hill.

The wind pitched her stiff body back and forth, but an inner drive pushed her on. She didn't understand what was happening, she didn't need to understand. The last thing she remembered was she was tipping back a celebratory glass of Pinot Grigio as she finished her first novel, and then, she woke up here.

The sporadic flashes of moonlight burned her eyes. She fondled her way through the centuries old cemetery. With each stiff, agonizing-step, she slowly had begun to understand that she was dead. Her mind swirled like the maelstrom whipping about her. It was like her body possessed . As if she were a slave of her own the dead flesh and the deep hunger was her Master.

As she reached the muddy road of the cemetery, she noticed she wasn't alone. She slowly craned her neck and saw she had at least twenty other similar figures following her. Something caught her attention. It was a scent. Her undead stomach growled, or at least seemed to, as she followed the urge.

The mustard colored rainstorm beat against her unfeeling body. She watched in childlike curiosity as the drops bounced off her skin, and then, she saw a figure kneeling next to a brown Chevy Chevette. The teenage driver was pulled off the main road in front of the cemetery entrance. The white glow of *The Pizza Shack* sign on the roof was lost within the swirl of the chaotic storm. It wasn't the aroma of pizza that attracted Carol, no; it was the racing pulse and throbbing heartbeat of the boy changing the flat tire on the small car.

She could hear him cursing as he spun the lug wrench. Every ounce of her being was filled with one thought and that was of a soul-tearing hunger. The driver thrashed about, and stood, and tossed the lug wrench into the hatch of the car as she came upon him. He jumped back into the hatch, and as the rain pounded down, she cried black tears as she and the others tore into his delicious flesh. She didn't want to bite the boy. She could feel what would have been her heart break as she let the warm blood and bits of tender flesh slide down her cold and taut throat. She felt as though she was watching a cheap horror movie, and while she never harmed a living thing in life, in death, all she wanted to do was devour the boy fighting to get away from her. With each and every bite, she cried inside to stop, but she couldn't.

"Hee...l.p," the kid cried out, and his words were lost in the storm.

Carol chomped down, again and again, relishing the tasty flesh. Cold tears streamed down her rotting cheeks, and she prayed to God to make her stop.

He didn't answer.

She finished the limp pizza delivery driver, rose, and headed toward the glowing lights farther on down the muddy access road.

It was only a few cold minutes before the ravaged teenager climbed up on shaky legs and she motioned for him to follow her.

21.

Precious and Grace
Route 14
Friday, 11:50 p.m.

Isandro sat next to the dead girl, staring at her young, dead face. Since they left the gas station, he found an overwhelming peacefulness in her wide, fear filled brown eyes fascinating. Her eyes were frozen in the moment of death, and he studied her. The gaping knife wound across her young throat reminded him of the dreams he'd had since he was a little kid. Demons coming to him at night—with their wide, smiling faces. Telling him to do very bad things to his family. The crescent shape of the gash in her neck mimicked the smiling hell spawned creatures. He had just laughed as she screamed and begged him to stop, but that never seemed to work. He ran his blood covered fingers gently over her cheek and explored the gaping wound. The dead teen's twin sister had screamed hysterically next to her, but Bobby made sure her mouth wouldn't let her make any noise for at least a little while.

There was something about her eyes and her face that he couldn't escape. He couldn't look away. The dilated orbs were calm as a lake's water in summer time, and he envied the girl. Her pale expression was soft and free of all tension. The weight of life was off of her. She would never have to feel pain again. This brutal world would never be able to shit on her again. No more doubt, no more fear, no more hating who she was. No more running. Nobody could ever hurt her again, or treat her like she was some insignificant piece of shit cockroach, and crush her dreams and her soul. No. Not her. Hell no, not EVER AGAIN!

89

Isandro gently pulled her into his chest and hugged her tightly. He softly kissed her sweat and blood matted hair.

"It's going to be okay," Isandro whispered like a ghost in the dead girl's ear, and then kissed it. He sipped from a tequila bottle and lightly brushed her dark hair from her face.

"You are free... At last." Isandro sipped and then kissed her head again.

"Sleep well, my sweet angel." He gave the slack body a final kiss and shoved her away from him like a rag doll a child was bored with. His expression hardened, all calmness was lost and washed away amongst the pounding of rain on top the speeding Cadillac.

"Hector, pull over," Isandro ordered, and drank deeply from the bottle, wiping the blade of the knife on the girl's bare leg.

His twin brother followed the order swiftly and pulled off onto the soft shoulder, into the cover of a row of low hanging willow trees. Isandro smiled wide at his brother's obedience. That's more like it, he nodded, and drank from the bottle.

"This should be good, bro," Hector said, putting the car into park. His words warbled and shook with doubt and fear. Isandro soaked in it and loved it.

"Yeah, we need to dump this bitch," Isandro said.

"Good idea," Hector said, and had to fight to open the door against the driving rain of the storm.

"What about this one?" Bobby asked. The girl's head was in his lap. He licked her cheek and grabbed a hold of her ass.

"Nah, hell no. We still have time to have some fun with the bitch." Isandro slapped the girl across the face and got out of the car behind his brother.

"Yo, Manny, white boy, grab that puta and get her out here," Isandro shouted into the car as a bright flash of lightning lit up the inside of the Caddy.

"On it, yo." Manny jumped out of the other side of the car, shoving Cahill forward into the dash as the sleepy white kid opened the door. "C'mon, cuz, what the hell?" Manny stopped and looked at Cahill, who was barely moving in the front seat.

"Sorry, yo, just draggin' ass, man. It's the damn tequila." Cahill tried to laugh it off. His words were soft and worn. Isandro heard the exchange and didn't really care. He just needed the putas to last until he found the Ranger and crossed the border. After that, they could all burn in hell, and he wouldn't care.

The raging storm, and its cruel yellow-tainted wind, battered at them, as the two bangers roughly yanked the dead teen from the backseat, dragging her white shoed feet to the back of the car. Just then, a wail of sirens and bright red and white light tore through the darkness of the night. They were parked off the road and under the cover of old willows, but it was nowhere near enough cover to hide the dead bitch from the row of cop cars bearing down.

"Ah, fuck me." Isandro sagged. He watched as what seemed like a damn parade of cop lights flash by them.

"Screw it. Toss the bitch in the trunk. We'll deal with it later," he said, drinking from the bottle.

"Where the hell is Cahill?" Isandro barked.

"His ass is busted, Boss. We got this," Manny quickly said, and grabbed the dead girl's ankles and hefted her up.

"Pussy." Isandro peered inside the car as if his red-hot glare could reach the passed out white boy.

"Nothin' but a thing, bro." Hector snatched up the girl by her armpits, and they callously tossed her slack, bloody body into the cold trunk of the Caddy.

"I'm hungry." Isandro's words were distant and cold. They all hopped into the car, away from the torrential storm, and pulled back onto the darkened highway.

"I'm thinking pancakes," Isandro said, sipping from the bottle, and wiping his hands clean on the dead girl's twin sister's Dallas Cowboy t-shirt.

"I think I know just the place," he added, and grabbed the girl by the back of her neck.

22.

What Are You Going to Do?
Rt. 14
Friday, 12:05 p.m.

"Where? What the hell, Ranger?" The girl was goddamn hysterical, and for Christ's sake, driving me bat-shit crazy. I was doing all I could to get my permanently side-ways head wrapped around what the Emergency Radio Broadcast had said. Damn, just a few short hours ago, I was on a plane with an asshole Governor and worried about losing my job and my family. Now, I'm driving down a pitch black highway in foul weather that would make Noah's rainstorm look like a fucking yard sprinkler.

"Just hold onto your damn pants." I shot her a look. It must have worked, because she shut up right quick, and looked fast out the window.

"Take a goddamn breath. Now, do me a favor, kid. Under your seat, should be two paper bags. Can ya fetch 'em for me, *por favor*?" My head was still reeling, and my throat was dryer than a fire ant's ass inside a volcano. I always had a backup.

"Uh yeah, sorry Ranger. But yo, dude, this shit is scary." Her tone was calmer, and she meant what she said. She reached under the seat and pulled out both bags. I knew I was going to need both before this whole night was over. She shook her head and handed them to me.

"No offense, but are you sure booze is the thing you need right now?" She straightened in her seat and stared at me. I returned the look, snatched the bottles from her hand, and placed the other bag on the seat beside me. I ignored her glare and returned to the black wash of road in front of us. The kid wasn't the first time I'd heard bitching about my drinking. Another McCutcheon legacy that I'd known for years I'd have to either deal with or die. I'd deal with the demon a different day.

"Don't you worry about me, girl." I shook the paper bag loose from the bottle of Jameson and let it fall to the floor. I jammed the bottle between my knees, and with my free hand, opened it. I chucked the cap into the backseat, grab the bottle, and took a long pull.

"And to answer your question, Jimbo's Rusty Cactus Diner," I told her between swigs and wiping the remainder on my jacket sleeve.

"What the hell is that?" she asked with a sharp edge to her voice.

"A diner. You asked me where we were going to go, and I'm fixin' to take us there." I drank a big mouthful of the brown liquid and let it work its mojo as it slid down my parched throat.

"Is it safe?" The tough teen seemed to melt into a little girl in the passenger seat, and I felt like shit. You calloused old fool. I cursed myself a few more times before I found the words.

"An old friend of mine owns it. He's a pecker-headed ol' jarhead like me. You'll be good to go, kid. Trust me, Stacy Jo, you have my word. I'll keep you safe." I offered her the most compassionate look I could muster. I was pretty damn sure it looked more like Frankenstein trying to smile than anything resembling comfort, but hell, it's what God gave me.

"You'd better, old man." She smiled weakly, grabbed the bottle from my hand, and took a shot that would have made some of my old Corps buddies proud. I nodded and quickly yanked my bottled 'spinach' back and smiled.

"Jimbo's good people, Kid. And if I know him, he'll have the place boarded up tighter than Fort Knox. He has more guns and ammo than the Texas National Guard and the whole lot of Rangers combined." The whiskey mixed with the acid in my throat as I forced both the booze and my words back down. I knew Jimbo was a worse drunk than I and would be goddamn lucky if he even had his radio on, much less battened down the hatches. The only prayer we had for safe haven was if Robbie was working. I said a prayer for such a thing as the New York kid and I shared the bottle of liquid courage.

I hoped it wouldn't run empty.

23.

Bad Girl
Jimbo's Rusty Cactus Diner & Blue Sky Drive-In
Rt. 14
Friday, 12:17 p.m.

As the Cadillac crested a rise, the dark veil of night was fractured by the bright glow of neon reds, white, and blue lights. Hector was blinded for a second and had to flip the visor down to shade his eyes.

"Motherfucker." He slowed the big car. Below them, set a wide valley, and off to the right, a glaring sign read: *Jimbo's Rusty Cactus Diner & Blue Sky Drive-in.* Beneath the old sign, the diner. It was a converted, old silver passenger car that used to take folks from Houston to New Orleans back when rail travel was all the rage. Now, it was one of the best roadside diners in all of Texas. The diner was small, and beyond its dirt parking lot, was one of the oldest drive-in movie theaters in the country. The Gate was chained shut, and the two large screens set dark and silent, entertaining only the driving rain, syncopated thunder, and lightning flashes.

"Oh hell yeah, esé. There it is." Isandro exhaled a cloud of smoke and laughed.

The crew began to stir as Hector drove slowly down the rain-slicked highway, toward the glowing sign that felt like it would burn out his already stressed retinas.

"The best fuckin' pancakes and sausage in the whole damn universe, yo." Isandro shoved the girl away. She'd fallen asleep a few miles back, and he'd moved onto more important things. He zipped his fly, took the final drag off the joint, and tossed it out the window.

"You sure this is the place you want to go, bro? Don't the pigs come here all the time?" Hector looked at his drunk, stoned brother through the rearview mirror.

"Don't worry about them assholes. Fuck 'em. They'll be too busy feeding their fat faces with donuts." Manny cackled, sipping from a bottle.

"Ain't afraid a no cop. You, brother?"

Hector could feel the cold stare of his brother in the rearview mirror, matched with a painful grip on his shoulder.

"'Sides, I got the munchies from hell, esé."

His brother's dark laugh sent chills through Hector's body, and when he didn't release his strong grip, Hector's gut told him all he needed to know.

The diner and drive-in came into view as he brought the car down the hill. Hector tried to swallow, and it felt as though he had a baseball with nails and screws impaled through it in his dry throat.

Hector was relieved to see only a few vehicles in the muddy parking lot. The old windshield wipers tried their best to keep the pounding rain at bay, but it wasn't going so good. Hector was actually glad they were stopping. With that fucked up news broadcast and this freaky weather, he quietly prayed for the end of the world.

He parked the Caddy at the end of the diner, by a dilapidated tall, palisade fence to the right, which housed the dumpsters and grease trap. He could hear the girl sobbing in her sleep from the backseat, and he said a prayer for her too.

"What we gonna do about—her?" he asked.

The girl cringed and started to scream and swing. Manny wrapped her in a big bear hug and squeezed. Hector heard all the air gush out her lungs. His chest tightened.

Isandro moved so fast, it startled Hector, and even Manny. His bloodstained hand roughly cupped the girl's sobbing mouth, while the other hand brandished a thin, long blade. He brought it to her trembling throat.

"Cahill, give me your jacket, yo." Isandro's voice was monotone, and his eyes never left the young girl's tear-filled face.

A long moment passed.

"Hey, asshole, wake the fuck up, esé!" Hector shoved the kid, who was sleeping in the passenger seat. He thought the kid was a dumb-ass, but he didn't deserve what Hector's psychotic brother would do to him if he didn't do as he was told. Hector gave him another shove, and the kid finally moved.

"What the hell, yo?" The kid's words were groggy and sounded as if they were coming from the grave—cold and distant—disconnected.

"Give Isandro your sweatshirt, man." Hector helped the kid take the shirt off, and Cahill didn't put up a fight. In fact, it seemed like he just went slack and let Hector do all the work. Hector didn't care, freed the jacked from the kid, and handed it over to his brother.

Isandro hadn't moved a muscle and was still staring into the girl's saucer-sized eyes.

The storm raged and battered the car, rocking it like they were at sea. It must have dropped at least ten degrees in the past hour. But, Hector found it oddly humid, and his breathing became labored.

Isandro's wrist flick was skilled and calculated. The blade sliced through the girl's jugular. He quickly wrapped the sweatshirt around her gushing throat and tied it off.

"What are you doin', Issie?" He couldn't hide his nerves. A harsh flash of lightning painted the interior of the car in a whitewash that was ruined by a spray of blood.

"Sshhhh. Sleep now. It's okay. Let go."

Hector heard his brother whisper in the dying girl's ear as he wiped the blade on her white cheek,

Hector wept.

Manny and Bobby watched with wide-eyed excitement, and drank from the bottles of liquor that still had blood smears on them. The girl's blood reminded Hector of when they were young and they watched football games on TV. He and Isandro would shake with anticipation as their favorite team would score a goal. That thought made him shiver, and he felt bile rush from his stomach to his throat. He fought the burning liquid back down, and wiped the tears from his aching eyes.

Isandro slowly turned his steely gaze at Hector. After a long chilling moment, he smiled wide, and brought a bottle of vodka to his lips.

"Takin' out the trash is all, brother." Hector saw absolutely nothing behind his eyes. They used to be so much alike. That was years ago. Now, sitting inside the Caddy filled with the smell of pot, booze, sex, and the coppery scent of blood, Hector hated himself for not seeing this coming years ago. He and his brother were nothing alike. He hated what Isandro had become, and even worse, he despised what he let himself become. His heart felt like it was filled with concrete, and so was his hope for a safe escape to Mexico. Hector and his brother stared into each other's eyes. Hector was certain that it was too late for him and most certain his brother was evil and would burn in Hell. All hope was lost. Hector let his body sag and shifted his weeping eyes away from his brother.

He wanted to cover his ears as Isandro's baleful laugh echoed, and the temperature dropped.

"Manny, you and this pendejo of a brother of mine, get rid of the *empties* behind the dumpsters and meet us inside. I need me some chow, yo." Isandro tucked a bottle into his jacket, got out of the car, and slammed the door.

Hector shook all over, and he no longer cared. Fuck the other gang-bangers in the car. He hoped they all died tonight. He prayed that whatever chemical or germ attack hit the east coast would come and wash them all away like the swirling storm outside.

Manny grabbed the girl and yanked her out the car. As fast as his large frame could manage, he dragged her out of sight of the diner's windows, toward the dumpsters. Hector met Bobby at the back of the car and didn't even look at the pudgy punk. He just opened the trunk lid, and the creak of its rusty hinges was lost in the thunder pounding above them.

Hector paused as the spastic bright flash of lightning bathed the immense trunk in its light, and the dead girl stared deeply into his bloodshot eyes. He knew she was dead. At least two hours gone. But her eyes bore deep into his soul and wrenched around like a knife cutting a deer. He pushed the painful thoughts out and prayed they'd wash away amongst the torrent.

He grabbed the teenager by the thin wrists and motioned for Bobby to get her ankles. They yanked the girl from her metal casket and out into the pouring rain. They moved quickly, robotically into the darkness of the dumpsters, and dropped the girl on top of her rigor-filled sibling.

Hector waved Manny and Bobby away. They turned, shaking their heads, laughing, and walked toward the front of the diner.

Hector fell to his knees into the mud and wept.

24.

El Loco
Inside Jimbo's Rusty Cactus Diner
Friday, 12:30 p.m.

The old bell jingled from the worn door as Isandro stepped inside. He was familiar with the railroad car diner. He remembered banging a bitch with tattoos in the bathroom, a year or so before his stint in Oklahoma. It still was a shit-hole, he mumbled, taking the bottle from under his jacket. The diner had a dated 50's décor, with all kinds of useless Army or Marine bullshit on the walls. Photos of pendejo Texas Rangers and other white boy assholes that Isandro would love to use for target practice. He was thinking about burning the roach trap to the ground, but decided he was far hungrier than anything else, so he filed that idea away. He did a fast check of the occupants and smiled.

He stood in the center of the diner. In front of him a long counter ran the length of it. Only one guy sat there. From the looks of his fat body, long hair, and ball cap, Isandro guessed he was a trucker. Nothing to worry about there. Off to the right, by the bathrooms, a young white boy with a smoking hot chica, were talking to a blonde, beehive-haired waitress. They looked like rich college kids. Must be on a date. "How fuckin' sweet." Isandro tasted the words and spat on the chipped, yellowing floor. The rest of the diner was empty. The place was all his. He sipped.

"Sit anywhere, hon. I'll be right with you," the short, pudgy waitress shouted, never looking at him or his crew.

He found a corner booth to his left that offered a complete view of his diner and plopped down on the end. Bobby and Manny sat down. Cahill walked like a damn zombie and nearly fell into the booth.

"Christ, holmes, you're a fuckin' lightweight." Manny slugged the pale kid in the arm. Cahill started to fall off the seat. Manny grabbed him and pulled him up.

"Yo, you gonna make it, bro?" Bobby asked.

Isandro just stared and drank from his bottle. He didn't even know why Hector brought him along in the first place. Kid was probably a rat from the DEA or ATF. Isandro felt the comfortable grip of his pistol and thought about putting a hole in the punk's face, right here and now. But again, his craving for pancakes and sausage outweighed his trigger finger. For now.

"Can't hang with the big boys, huh, esé?" Manny laughed, and patted the kid on the back. Cahill almost slid onto the floor again, but Manny yanked him up by his sweat and blood-soaked covered wife-beater.

"Shit, yo, take your nasty white ass to the shitter 'n wipe that funk off of ya." Bobby pinched his nose closed and laughed loudly.

"Yeah, you smell like Bobby's mamma's coochie." Manny laughed and held out a hand for Isandro to high-five, but it was left hanging. Manny dropped it quickly.

"Fuck you, asshole." Bobby shot Manny a sharp look.

Cahill suddenly jumped up from the booth and ran toward the bathroom.

"Heh, see, told ya. Your mamma's snatch is nasty enough to make ya puke." Bobby slapped Manny across the back, and they began to wrestle in the booth.

Isandro sat back and drank from his bottle, caressed the wooden grip of his pistol, and felt his stomach growl for pancakes. He could hear the Voice talking again.

The *Voice* had been his best friend since before he could walk. He found it comforting, but scary as all hell at the same time. It started small and told him to do things. Bad things. Violent things, like stomping on ants or tearing off flies and bees wings. He really liked doing that. When he got older, the *Voice* encouraged him to see what was inside the stomach of local cats and dogs. He really, really enjoyed doing that. When he was twelve, he and Hector cornered some retarded kid from the next shit town over, walking through their hood. The *Voice* commanded him to teach the '*tard* a lesson. Isandro watched and knew his puta of a brother was faking it. Hector threw a few pansy-assed punches, but wimped out. When the *Voice* whispered into Isandro's ear, he followed the command. Hector just stared, eyes wide, and mouth hung open.

It made Isandro laugh. But not as much as when he followed the Voice's orders and slit open the dumb-ass kid's throat with a broken Coke bottle. Isandro made his brother help him dump the body in Old Man Rojas's pigpen. The fat bastards made short work of the retard. His loser brother went home, but it was okay, because Isandro and the *Voice* watched with excited eyes and approving smiles as the pigs relished in their midnight snack.

The *Voice* had become Isandro's constant companion. It always spoke to him when he was the most lost. The dark, smooth voice talked his damn ear off while in prison. Non-stop. Every day, he was lucky if he could get an hour of straight sleep each night. Isandro hated the *Voice* at first, but then it began to tell him things. Wise things. Whenever he couldn't make a decision or had a hard choice to make. That usually included the times he'd take care of a fellow member that went off the reservation and had to be dealt with. In the dark moments when he was filled with doubt and had deep feelings of weakness, the *Voice* spoke to him the loudest. The *Voice* always knew just what to do.

The memory of the time back in Nacogdoches, when the word came down from the Perez Cartel in Mexico City, that a fucking rat had infiltrated the organization. It was Manuel Santos, that Isandro had sponsored into the gang and was about to be *jumped in*. It turned out that the pendejo prick was an undercover Texas fucking Ranger. That kind of betrayal and loss of trust meant a death sentence for the cop and his sponsor—Isandro. He knew he was a walking dead man, and he had to do something. He felt betrayed. He'd trusted Santos, and they'd become brothers. Done things that he was damn sure as a cop, the dude shouldn't have done. He even brought the bastard into his home for Christmas dinner with his family. Isandro was furious, but torn. His mind swirled with anger, disbelief and fear. He actually was considering letting the asshole off the hook, and was going to talk to the Cartel and see if there wasn't a mistake or another way of handling things. That's when the Voice bellowed.

Kill the worthless puta. Do it now! The Voice repeated the cold words for twenty-four hours straight. He knew the Voice was right.

The pendejo Ranger was laughing and drinking in his back yard having a Fourth of July picnic with his family, along with a handful of other off-duty Rangers, when Isandro and his crew crashed the party.

The *Voice* shouted in his drug-rattled mind. *Kill them... Kill them ALL!*

The news reported later that night, that twenty-four people had been brutally slain at the Santo's residence. Amongst the dead were four children ranging from six months to eight years of age. It was also reported the Ranger's tongue, eyes, and heart were missing. That made Isandro smile, and he knew then and there the Voice always spoke the truth. It was that little incident which sent the other asshole Ranger, McCutcheon, after Isandro's ass. Hell, Isandro was honored that he was the sole target of the Rangers. But it was McCutcheon that seemed to have a big hard-on for him. He didn't know and didn't give a rat's ass either. He was just another puta the Voice would tell him to butcher like the pig he was. Isandro let the words warm him. They always made things so simple. He liked simple.

The words came again. Soft, at first, then quickly rising in timbre and intensity. The Voice filled his thoughts and were quickly jolted away, as a round of thunder shook the diner. He found his hand gripping the pistol tightly. He was starving for pancakes, but he knew the Voice had a hankering from something a little more...bloody.

The bleach-blonde waitress walked toward them, and Isandro's mouth split into a wicked smile. The old bitch made her way to his booth. Just the way Isandro liked them.

"Sorry, hon, been one hell of a night." Her face was tired, and her makeup was worn off. She was covered in sweat. Isandro laughed as she adjusted her beehive hairdo and chomped on a wad of gum. "What can I get for ya?" She never looked at him or the other crew in the booth.

"Yo." He leaned in to read her name tag. *Robbie.* "I'll take the biggest stack of pancakes you got and a shit-ton of bacon... Keep 'em comin'." He leaned back, pulled out his bottle, and sipped from it, never losing his smile.

The *Voice* grew louder.

He wondered what her insides looked like.

Not looking up from her notepad, she said, "You want some coff... Oh." Her gaze caught the bottle in his hand, and she quickly turned to Manny and Bobby and took their orders. Isandro was too busy listening to the sinister words rolling around his maelstrom-filled mind.

The waitress finished, gave him a weak smile, and waddled back toward the kitchen. She passed the two lovebirds sitting at the far end of the diner. They were barely twenty, if that. The pasty white dude wore a University of Houston t-shirt and blushed while talking to the blonde bitch sitting across from him. They think they're so goddamn smart. The *Voice* growled. They had books splayed out in front of them, and Isandro had noticed they'd shot Cahill ugly looks as he ran past them, on his way to the bathroom. *Snobby, college fucks,* he thought, and found himself wanting to explore their arrogant bellies as well.

"What ya thinkin', Boss?" Manny asked, looking anxious.

"Time to go back to school." The Voice came out through his mouth. He nodded with a wide grin at the co-eds flirting and eating onion rings.

Manny, and Bobby, turned and watched the couple play grab ass for a couple minutes before turning back to Isandro with the same twisted grins on their faces. Manny licked his lips and drank from his bottle.

"What ya thinking?" Manny bounced with excitement.

Isandro lived for that.

"School's out forever." Isandro laughed, his fist closed tightly and dragged his outstretched thumb across his throat. He knew that Manny would understand. The kid must be hearing the same voice. He would be a good replacement for his number two. He sipped the bottle, and waited for the pancakes and floorshow to begin.

The *Voice* was growing louder and very impatient.

***

Outside Jimbo's Diner

Hector's world was torn apart. He'd been his twin brother's protector, defender, and best friend. Especially inside the *Los Malvados.* Hector and Isandro grew up on the bloody, violent streets. The gang offered safety and a purpose. But it also rife with backstabbing, treacherous scumbags. The gang was packed with feral dogs, all fighting to be the alpha. Hector never failed to back any of Isandro's many plans. Even the ones he didn't fully agree with. But brothers always back each other's plays. Their Papi taught them that at a young age, and Hector never forgot it.

But here, knee deep in mud, in front of two dead, innocent girls that his brother had slaughtered without hesitation, Hector was lost. The storm was fierce, and the rain felt like a million tiny shards of frozen glass boring into his cold skin. His chest burned, and his tears mixed with the rain. Every inch of his body was filled with pain and felt like dead weight.

He'd done everything for his twin. He'd betrayed, stole, cheated, and even had killed people for him. All in hopes that Isandro would come back to Mexico with him and they could leave the damn gang behind—find a new life somewhere— anywhere. He thought Isandro wanted to get out of the gang life, but he was wrong. It was loud and clear that he loved every sick, twisted part of it. There was nothing he could do to change his dark mind.

Hector's sobs rocked him, and the storm railed on. The two girls stared at him with wide, death-filled eyes. He had to do something. He didn't care if he got killed trying, but he had to do something. This wasn't right. This wasn't the way they were raised.

His body felt like a hundred sandbags were tied to him, but he managed to climb up from the mud hole, next to the dumpster, and looked up at the ebony sky above him.

"Dios mio. Mamma, Papi, forgive me." He closed his eyes and prayed for the first time in years.

He turned, started toward the diner, but stopped. He looked down at the girls; their bloodied, bruised bodies lay in a twisted mass of limbs. His heart ached. His soul burned with sorrow, shame, and horror. He made the sign of the cross, mouthed the words, "I'm sorry," and gripped the cold steel of the .38 Special tucked inside the back of his waistband.

A bright flash of lightning startled Hector as he turned back to the diner. He slogged through the mud; never noticing the slight twitches of movement of the twin girls heaped against the rusty dumpster.

25.

Avalon Hideaway
Inside Jay McCutcheon's 'Cuda

The rain was thicker than mud as we topped the hill above the small valley that was home to my good buddy, Jimbo's diner. I knew this area like the back of my hand. I'd spent most of my time here, growing up, and as a Ranger. Even shit-faced off my gourd and dead-ass tired, I could find my way here, even if it was through a yellow-piss colored rainstorm. Whatever the biological attacks were, I was pretty damn certain that good ol' Jimbo would have his shit wired tight and the diner would be secure. I hoped.

The blinding white and yellow of the sign welcomed us as I drove down the hill.

"What the hell?" Stacy Jo yelled, covering her eyes.

I laughed, sipped from my bottle. "That would be Jimbo's Diner, kiddo. He never was a guy for subtlety." I shook my head and descended the rain-slicked hill. Despite the raging storm, Jimbo's sign lit up a good three acre-parcel of the highway surrounding his joint. I slowed the car as we approached the parking lot and took stock. I thought I saw something moving in the darkness around the diner, but the way the lightning was flashing like a damn strobe-light, I couldn't be sure. And I really didn't think anyone in their right mind would be out for a stroll in this shit.

An old blue and red Kenworth tractor trailer with a piggy-backed load set at the far end of the lot, while a dented up Dodge pick-up, and a small white Honda, set in front of the diner. The only other car in the muddy lot was a long Caddy that reminded me of one of Elvis's rides or something from the Munster's TV show I watched as a kid. I chuckled as I pulled in next to it and put the car into park.

"Wonder if the King's in for a *peanut butter and 'nana sandwich?*" I did my best Elvis impersonation. Stacy Jo just looked at me as if I had sprouted a third ear out my forehead and I'd spoken Martian. I shook my head, took a swig from the bottle, and shrugged.

"I told you, kiddo. You'll be safe here. You hungry? Jimbo makes the best damn pancakes in the world. I swear." She looked none-too-impressed. *Goddamned kids these days*, I bitched to myself, shut the car off, and got out. I instinctively felt the grip of my service weapon and the knife strapped to my belt while I looked out at the muddy parking lot. I knew Jimbo would have plenty of food, but I still had to try and sell the whole *'It's safer than Fort Knox'* thing to the kid, just to keep things cool. There was some truth to what I told her. James Joseph Ferguson was one bad ass Marine. But that was years ago. The booze and long list of ex-wives had cleaned his clock. And while it's gospel that the man can make a killer pancake, he is nuttier than a shit house rat. There was no way in hell I was going to tell this to Stacy Jo. The small lie would have to do.

She reluctantly got out of the car. "Yeah, pancakes do sound good," she said as she closed the door, her wide, blue eyes taking in the entirety of Jimbo's Diner. Something told me that she was looking for more than the best seat in the house.

I was starting to like this kid.

Shoot me now.

I made my way up the front steps of the old train car-turned diner and actually felt my stomach growl. Maybe coming here was a good idea after all. I'd lost a lot of faith in my gut hunches lately, but the food sounded good.

I should have listened to my gut.

26.

World of Swirl
Inside stall #2
Jimbo's Diner

Cahill crashed to his knees. Brown and yellow liquid painted the inside of the toilet bowl. His gut and throat were afire as his body shook the contents of his stomach loose. He felt like he was dying. Every inch of his thin frame shook uncontrollably—shooting with ungodly pain and torment. His teeth clicked and clacked together so hard he'd thought they would shatter. The agony burst from the bite from the old fucking man back at the roadstop. It radiated out, and with each inch, ripped at him until it reached his sweat-soaked feet. When he was eleven he had pneumonia, and he thought that was the worst he ever felt. His skin was hot to the touch, and it felt like he'd been swimming in the Evart's pool. His neighbors cared a hell of a lot more about him than his own parents did. They were the ones who took him to the hospital. He felt like the Incredible Hulk had beaten him repeatedly with a baseball bat. That was ten years ago and a million miles away. Cold, darting jolts of pain ripped through his shuttering body, and he knew he was truly dying. Laying here in some shit-hole bathroom, he did something he hadn't done on a long time. Between jerking spasms of agony and violent puking, he prayed to a God he'd abandoned long ago. Tears fell down his burning skin, and a gusher of blood erupted from his mouth and anus; he hoped the God hadn't forgotten about him.

He collapsed on the cold, blood and feces covered floor, silent prayers still working on his lips. Jason Marshall Cahill, bled out, and died.

Reanimation came to Cahill in a jolting rush. Like he was rocketing down an enclosed log flume, just like the one he'd seen at Ten Points Amusement Park in Irving. His mind violently sped toward a pinprick of light at the end. No colors, just a burning intense, white light.

The next of his senses to come swirling back was his hearing. Rain pounded the thin roof of the diner. It reminded him of his small bedroom in his parent's trailer. They were dirt poor, and the trailer was barely livable. The town's code enforcement officer had actually threatened to condemn the matchbox on wheels a few times. But that stopped when Cahill's step-dad kicked the dog shit out of the book wormy dude, and he never came back after that. Cahill's ceiling was basically a piece of old particleboard, covered with old corrugated tin sheet. When it rained, it sounded like all those war movies his step-dad used to watch, that was after he slapped the hell out of him. It was this memory of the pounding rain, and how he would hide from the goddamn drunk and the constant, *ting-ting-ting* of rain on the tin roof that helped him push the real world out.

As the twisting, turning ride continued, feeling returned to Cahill's freezing body. Pain ruled every square inch of the dead teen. The bite from the old man was the source of the pain. But it was no longer isolated agony. Daggers of fire tore through each and every bone in his cold body. Every inch of his skin burned with a cold fire. The very marrow of his bones ached like they were filled with broken glass. Every muscle stiffened and felt like he weighed a thousand pounds. The only feeling not returning was his heartbeat. He was dead, and that stark realization made him weep. He wanted to wipe the ice-cold tears from his frozen cheeks, but his limp arms refused to move. The blackness whipped past as the pinprick of light grew closer. Now looking like a distant sun.

Cahill's death's log flume ride sped up, and with every bone wrenching second closer to the light he raced, the colder he became. The pain began to recede. Like water after a flood. In its wake, it left desolation and despair. Waterlogged memories and cold, bloated death, as the white light engulfed him. The flood of death washed every aspect of Cahill away, save two emotions that the vile reaper allowed him to carry with him in his new unlife.

The overwhelming need to feed... Feed on human flesh. The second was the ironic brutal awareness that what he was ravenous for was wrong.

His hunger drove Cahill slowly to his wobbly legs and forced out a low groan. He fell against the sink, his undead arms barely kept him from bashing his head on the hard ceramic. He forced himself up and caught a glimpse of the thing he'd become in the dirty, smeared mirror. It wasn't the face of a dead man that ripped his soul out, no... it was the black tears that rolled down his pale cheeks and the black, empty eyes that ushered them into this cold new world he now existed in.

The moment of horror quickly passed as an aching in his stomach and brain told him it was time. Time to feed, and there was a glorious buffet waiting for him, just outside the bathroom door.

He thought he heard his undead stomach growl, but his drive to eat was coming from a far darker...far more evil source. He clumsily turned and willed his stiff legs to move. It was like trying to move two one hundred pound bags of cement. The doorway to warm, succulent flesh was only a mere five feet away. Cahill had no doubt his new, insatiable hunger would provide him the energy he needed. The thought of actually eating human flesh made him want to vomit, and his heart broke every time he imagined it. But it was hastily wiped away by the more dominant urge. He surrendered to it, and with all his might, shambled his left leg one step closer to the door.

The sweet smell of the living wafted through the thin door. His undead face broke into a grotesque smile as he staggered one step closer.

27.

Got Me Under Pressure

I heard the old familiar ring of that stupid bell that Jimbo insisted added *ambience* to his four-star eatery. His words, not mine. Screw that. To me, it was a fucking pain in the ass, and I threatened to yank the damn thing off the wall every time I came in the joint. This time, it didn't seem that important. The storm was kicking the black Texas landscape something fierce, and with that emergency broadcast about some insane terrorist attacks, I had a hell of a lot more on my mind than some doorbell Jimbo picked up at Garrett's Hardware for five goddamn dollars. The brightness of the diner was a welcomed sight. It had been a long day, and with thoughts of Inez weighing heavy on my mind, the New York kid tagging along, for Christ's sake, I needed some food, a stiff drink, and to take a piss. Even though it seemed the world was swirling down the shitter, Jimbo's was just the right place. I still needed to get home to Inez and Bellia, but here, I could at least get some chow for me and the girl, call Inez, and make sure they are both okay.

An old black and white TV rested atop a rusty old Coca Cola machine, with its volume turned off. On the fuzzy screen, a local cheap dress jacketed clown gave what appeared to be a current update about the attacks or some shit. I just needed to clear my head and call my girls. The apocalypse could fucking wait.

The jukebox played George Jones's, *"Hell Stays Open All Night,"* as I looked around. There were only a handful of people inside the diner. A trucker, named Whitney, I'd seen a bunch of times. A good guy, but talked more bullshit than Carter had liver pills. A couple of college looking kids talking nervously to two Mexican tough guys. I filed that away. And to the left was a lone guy, sitting at the far end of the diner. He had a hood over his eyes and sat slumped. I filed that away too.

Take a goddamn day off, asshole. I never listen.

"So, are we gonna sit down or are you wrestling with redecorating choices?" The girl shoved past me and plopped into the first booth to my right.

"Smart ass," I said, shaking my head. I followed suit, sat down opposite her, and took my hat off, placing it on the table. I was tired, worn out, and stressed beyond imagination. I was sure the attacks happening on the east coast and over in Europe would be contained with minimal damage. My time in the Corps had trained me, and while I had some issues, I still had faith in our leaders. Whatever *this* was, in the end, they'd take care of it, and we'd be good. I was far more worried about my fiancé and baby girl—if they'd even be home when I got there. I felt for my bottle and smiled when my shaking hand found its comforting glass.

"Well holeee-sheeeit. Be still my aching heart. Look what the storm dragged in." Robbie approached with a broad smile on her tired face.

I smiled in return. I liked Robbie. She was a good woman who deserved a hell of a lot more than what Jimbo kept promising her. He was an old dog, and I knew without a damn doubt he would never learn any new tricks.

"How you been, darlin'?" I asked.

"Glory be, let me make sure my old eyes are seeing right. Yup... Yes sir, that be one and only Texas Ranger, Jay McCutcheon, sitting in my section." She bellowed the words in her smooth yet, sarcastic way.

I just shook my head, waved her off and laughed. I held my hand out for a menu, which I already knew by heart.

A flurry of motion caught my attention. It was the Mexican thugs that I saw when I came in. The first class scumbags were messing with the couple seated by the bathrooms. The fat one offered me a crooked smile. I filled it away. I kept my eye on them overtop the menu.

"So, where the hell have you been, sexy?" Robbie chomped her gum like a cow chews its cud and winked. "You stepping out on me?" She shot Stacy Jo a glance. Chomping even harder.

"Hells no, Robbie. I came back just to see your sweet ass." I shot her a wink and caught Stacy Jo rolling her eyes, making a gagging gesture with her finger.

She bellowed a belly laugh, and even Stacy Jo let out a short chuckle. Robbie was painfully infectious that way.

"Ohhhhhh, I bet you say that to all the gals, you velvet tongue-devil." Robbie laughed again, tapping the girl on the shoulder with her order pad, and giving her a nod.

"I do, actually." I laughed. She smacked me with her notepad and giggled. It was forced.

I filed it away—an old cop habit. Another one, dying hard.

"So, seriously, I was driving from DFX, and then a storm from Satan's anus was on my trail. I figured, if we all were going to that *great greasy spoon in the sky*, no better place in the world than Jimbo's armpit diner to bite the big'n." I knew we both were ignoring what was going on outside, she needed to hear my usual charming conversation. Now was not the time to panic.

"So, enough with the ass-grabbing, Ranger. Who might this sweet young filly be?" she asked, raising a penciled on eyebrow at me. I knew where she was going and needed to cut her off quick like.

"This here is Sta…"

"Nikki Prince." The girl cut me off, her face flushed. She took the menu Robbie offered her, and she wouldn't look at me. This girl was tough and smart. Not using her real name was a wise move for someone on the run. How the hell did I even know if Stacy Jo was her real name? Her real name aside, I hated to tell her, no matter how far or fast she ran, there are just some demons you can never outrun, now wasn't the time.

"Well, Nikki, it's a pleasure." Robbie handed the girl the menu, all the while looking at me with that arching, inquisitive eyebrow. She knew I was engaged and all about Inez and the baby.

"Ah hell, Robbie. The kid was stranded at Moe's, needed a ride, so I helped her out. Quit looking at me like that for fuck's sake." I turned my full gaze on her and pulled my bottle out from under the table. "Can't I do a good deed every now 'n again? I am a cop, after all," I added with just the right amount of half buzzed indignation.

Robbie flailed her arms about in a 'No offense' gesture and winked at me. "That's true. You are a blessed angel of mercy, Ranger. A godsend indeed." She laughed and even coaxed another small giggle from the wise-ass New York kid.

"He's been a true gentleman, ma'am," Stacy Jo, Nikki, whatever her damn name was, added with a wide grin.

"Well, that's good to hear. Once upon a time young lady, good ol' James here was a real lady-killer. And even though it's hard to see now, he was actually quite the looker in his prime." Robbie was beside herself with laughter, slapping the pad against her leg. She was a damn laugh riot.

"Ha, you're one to talk, old woman. Haven't you've been a dish-jockey since Jesus was a mess cook?" I was feeling the effect of booze, stress, and the shit-storm awaiting me at home. My humor was a bit off. To make up for it, I took another sip.

"So, you gonna order something to eat or you just going to have your usual liquid dinner?" She was still chortling, but her shift in tone of voice was warning me she was changing into *Mother* mode.

"You sure you don't work weekends in Vegas, smart ass?" I grinned, sipped, and looked at her. Robbie had been a waitress at the Rusty Cactus Diner since Jimbo opened the place after he got out of the Corps, and her tired face wore every year since on it. She and Jimbo had been an on-again-off-again thing since the first day. Neither one of them were the settling down kind. They were perfect for each other. I liked her. She'd been a big help through all of my issues and never gave up on me. I cut her some slack when it came to constantly busting my balls with a sledgehammer.

"What? And take a huge pay cut and lose the glory of defending our great country?" I laughed, and after one of Robbie's patented, *I'll kick you in the nuts*, looks, I decided I should order. "Yeah, yeah. Give me the Dino- Pulled Pork and some onion rings." I handed the menu to her.

"Something to drink? Besides whiskey, if you please." She glared at me, with a holier-than-thou expression, over the top of her glasses perched on the tip of her short nose.

Not hesitating, I said, "Milk, please and thank you." I returned her smile.

She turned to the kid, shaking her head all the while. "For you, young lady?"

"Um...Just some water would be great." Stacy Jo's face flushed. I could see her trying to be sneaky, feeling around her pants pockets and stalling.

I knew she must be hungry, but too proud to ask for help. I hated even more that I liked this kid.

I lightly tapped Robbie's worn shoe with my boot, and we exchanged a knowing glance.

"Oh, honey, we're having an end-of the world special. Everything on the menu is free." Robbie must have been dead-ass tired, because that was the worst move I've ever seen her make. Stacy Jo wasn't a fool and knew exactly what the less-than crafty waitress was trying to do.

"You're about as subtle as a bull in a goddamn china shop, Rob." I laughed.

Robbie's face turned to the color of the Heinz Ketchup bottle on the table.

"Nah, it's okay. I'm not that hungry," Stacy Jo lied.

"It's on me. Besides, according to Ms. End-of-Days here, it could be out last meal. Eat," I said.

Stacy Jo flicked me a quick look and a faster smile. "Thanks. I'll have the *Tres Hombres* Special. With a Mountain Dew, please." She handed the menu back to Robbie. Lightning flashed. They all jumped like a bunch of nervous nancys.

"That's some shit kicking out there tonight," Robbie said. "How's the roads?"

"Like riding on icy rails, Rob. Hell, it's the only reason I stopped. Otherwise, I'd be almost home by now. It's nothing like I've seen before. I'm surprised the state hasn't shut the roads down." I sipped from my bottle and ignored Robbie's derisive looks.

A bolt of lightning struck a nearby tree and its sister; thunder added an exclamation point on the attack. It served to suck all the light hearted chatter out of the diner and refocus us on what the hell was going on outside the wind-assailed diner.

"They have, darlin'. About an hour ago, the Texas state transportation secretary issued a no travel advisory. Least, that's what I thought he said. Hard to tell since old numb-nuts back there in the kitchen insists on keeping the TV's sound off." She grimaced, tucking her order pad into her stained apron.

"Ah, hell." I took another pull from the whiskey bottle and peered through the yellow curd covering the diner's already dirty windows.

"I'll let you two love birds catch up. I need to use the little wrangler's room," Stacy Jo said with a nervous look over my shoulder.

Robbie giggled. "Oh, it's at the back of the diner, sweetheart. Take a left at the pay phone. Otherwise, you'll be peeing in the parking lot." She pointed to her left, still giggling.

The anxious kid slid out of the booth, quickly heading in the direction of the bathrooms.

Once out of earshot, Robbie leaned into me, and said,

"I like her. She reminds me of I—"

"Inez? I know. She's a tough kid," I admitted.

"What's her story?" Robbie's tired eyes followed the young girl as she reached the pay phone hanging on the wall and turn.

"Not sure. All I know is she's a runaway from upstate New York. That's all she told me. Well, that and she has family in Mexico." I drank and wiped my mouth on my sleeve as the storm punched at the diner.

"What happened up at Moe's?" Robbie leaned against the table.

"She was at the bus station there, used the pay phone and walked outside. I guess she was waiting for a ride. But some of those Arian, scumbag K.S.O. bikers and their old ladies followed her out to the parking lot. And I had to, well...ya know." I let the words hang out there and drank.

"Always the knight in shining armor, ain't you, Jay? Never take a day off, do you?" Robbie's words held a mix of admiration and concern.

I shrugged. "Never said I was smart." I looked deep into the brown liquid spinning in the bottle. White light splashed across it through tinted windows.

Again, in her nosey, but motherly way, she asked, "How's things with you an Inez? I know you two have had a tough go of it lately."

"Things have been good. But, there was an issue on the job today, which is why I need to get my ass back to Houston as soon as we're done eating here." I took in the raging storm and wondered if traveling was a good idea. But I was never one who listened to common sense. Maybe that was half my problem. At least that's what the Shrink back at headquarters had written in my file. But tonight, I needed to fix things and fix them now. The storm of the century, terrorist attacks, and Apocalypse be damned. Come hell or high water, I would be getting to Houston before daylight.

"Oh no. Not again, Jay?" She used the same condescending, but well-meaning tone she always used when I fucked things up. Tonight was not the night. I loved the woman, but her smothering, nursemaid shit was the last thing I needed. I took a long pull and shot her a look that I was damn sure she couldn't misunderstand. She straightened, and her face when slack, she knew.

"Sorry. I'll give Jimbo your order. I'm sure he'll be happy to see you."

Her face was far redder than the ketchup bottle. I instantly regretted the way I glared at her and felt like a world-class piece of shit.

She meant well. She always does. It was just that I was getting damn tired of beating myself up. I didn't need anyone else helping my quick decline into the dark realms of self-loathing and pity-goddamn-parties. I tried to stop her and apologize, but she was already passed the college kids.

Dammit it, McCutcheon, I cursed myself. The marathon of fucked-up-ness continued. I grabbed the bottle, stood up, and fumbled through my pockets for change. The whiskey was working its Irish magic as I walked to the pay phone. I needed to call Inez and make sure she was okay. The storm, the terrorists attacks, my fucking up like a royal jackass, yeah, that warranted a phone call. I'd left the last call to help the young girl. How the hell was I going to explain that? It always seemed like I spent most of my time explaining myself. Jesus Christ. What a mess I'd made of my life. I sipped, place the bottle on top of the phone, and picked up the receiver. I filched a handful of coins from my pocket and dumped them next to the bottle. A few coins toppled on the floor. I let them go.

I put a few quarters in the slot and dialed home. Next to the phone, a door looked out over the rain-soaked parking lot. The lightning and thunder were a constant dark song and dance. Yellow mist swirled and attacked the diner. I peered out into the dismal storm, the swaying winds, and relentless rain.

The phone connected and began to ring. Its tone seemed cold and distant. It rang and rang. She's probably gone. Took Bellia and headed south, across the border.

Finally, it picked up.

The sound of my own voice spoke to me through the crackling lines.

"Goddammit." I wanted to smash the receiver through the window. Instead, I slammed it back into the cradle and drank. My eyes burned looking out into the storm.

My stomach rolled, and I knew I had to get back on the road. The hell with the food, I needed to get out of there and back home. I stared out into the darkness, and I could have sworn I saw something out there. Something or someone—moving in the rain. Maybe it wasn't the rain and wind that was swaying and swerving after all. Maybe it was the booze, or being dog-tired, but I could have sworn I saw a shit-load of people walking out in the storm. Realizing that it was just the day from hell for me, I took a pull from the bottle, chalked it up to me being a drunk, paranoid idiot, and let it go. I was finally going to take a damn day off. I needed to take care of me and mine for a change. The kid could catch a ride here. Maybe Whitney could give her a ride. He was always heading into Mexico on deliveries. Either way, I'd done my good deed. She wasn't my problem anymore. Filled with a newfound conviction, the whiskey somehow tasted sweeter. I nodded and tried to forget about the moving storm outside.

"Atten-hut! Officer on deck!"

A deep, booming voice jolted me. I jumped, knocking both the coins from atop the phone, almost pissing my pants.

I spun, ready to make someone's day pretty shitty.

Fucking, Jimbo.

28.

Keep My Heart in a Rage.

The *Voice* raged inside Isandro's head.

Kill the pendejo motherfucker. And that bitch that's with him too! The Voice shouted and repeated its command, as Isandro watched the stocky man in the long leather jacket and Stetson hat sitting only a mere thirty feet away from him.

It was as if Jesus Christ himself, who Isandro had thought forsaken his sorry ass a long time ago, was sending him a peace offering. He couldn't believe the blessing that was set before him. At last, God and his Son finally were bowing down to him? It was only fitting, as he was, Isandro Philippe Dianira, god living among mortals. He drank from his bottle, and a wicked, crooked grin broke across his face. Judgment day was upon the world. He licked his lips, felt the grip of his pistol, and the grin sliced into a wide smile as he watched the drunken Ranger stagger to the pay phone.

A gift from God it was. Manny and Bobby stared at him like he was fucking loco. He was far from crazy. No, he had never been clearer. His mind was swirling with ideas, and his moment of revenge was at hand. He was certain he couldn't lose, considering God himself had laid the Ranger, who had destroyed his life, at his doorstep. Maybe the wailing storm outside and the attacks they talked about on the radio were true signs from God that it was the end of days, and that he was the sword of God. Sent to cleanse the world of vile creatures like this puta with the hat. It was a good place to start.

29.

It's so Hard.

Jimbo wrapped his muscular, hairy arms around me, and squeezed. The bear hug forced the air from my lungs. His face was filled with a broad, white smile. His chubby cheeks deep with dimples were the color of roses. The jarhead turned grill-jockey still had the looks of the same eighteen-year-old I met at boot camp. Lucky bastard.

"Damn good to see ya, man." Jimbo smiled and hugged me tighter.

Forcing the words out, "Can't...brea," I gasped.

"Ah hell. Sorry, Jay." Jimbo released me, and I wheeled back. Thank God, the pay phone broke my fall.

"It's okay, brother." I laughed, catching my breath. "It's damn good to see ya too, hoss." I said, slapping the big man on his shoulder. We were like brothers. We'd been through the mosquito-infested swamps and hell-spawned Drill Sergeants of Paris Island and saved each other's ass in Viet Nam. We were true Devil-Dogs through and through, surviving both the Tet Offensive and the fall of Saigon. We left that hell-hole on the same bird. Like I said, we were brothers. But that still didn't explain Jimbo's over emotional hug. Hell, we weren't in the damn Navy, what's with the hug? Am I dying and didn't know it? Jimbo had always been a little sensitive, quite the contrast with his brutish size. Damn, I'd seen the man clear an entire barroom of drunken Army pukes by himself. But damn... It was just weird.

"What the hell you doing out in this shit? You on duty?" he asked, adjusting the grease-stained, Dallas Cowboy's baseball cap on his sweaty, round head.

"Nah. I'm headed home. I had some shit detail up in Lubbock." I pulled the bottle from the top of the pay phone and offered him a sip.

He eyed the bottle, and after a long moment, he took it, sipped, and then handed it back. He had a strange look on his face. Like he was constipated or something. He wanted to speak, but it was stuck.

"How is the new duty going?" he asked. His face continued to squirm.

"It's going all right," I lied. I studied his eyes, and they danced around, looking everywhere but my face. Something was up.

"Jimbo, what the hell's going on, man?" I held my arms out wide and forced him to look into my eyes.

The storm continued its furious assault on the diner. Adding more drama to the annoyingly awkward scene inside. That big-ass Mexican was still shooting me looks, which normally would be enough reason for me to stomp a mud-hole in his ass, but now was not the time. But, if they kept messing with those young college kids, I just might have to say *hello*.

"Hell, Jay." Jimbo hung his head and stepped closer. "Sorry, man. It's just that Robbie and me, we've been talking to Inez, and she's been worried about you. With you're drinking, fighting at work. You're a damn time bomb, brother."

He glimpsed up at me, looking for my telltale sign of anger. But it must have been off duty, because he continued talking without a shattered jaw.

"Ya know that I love ya, and I would never stick my nose in your business, but, Robbie said you came in with some young girl. What...I...with what happened before, I jus—"

I cut him off.

"You kidding me, man? You're the one guy I thought understood me." I stepped back, and my first impulse was to shatter the bottle over his head. But I held that thought off. I took a deep breath. Held it, and let it out slowly.

"Jim. Now look. I know I've screwed things up in the past, and I am a hell of a way from perfect. But man, I love Inez, you know that. And with baby Bellia here, she means the world to me. I wouldn't do anything to mess that up, my brother. I swear." I grabbed his face and pulled it close to mine. I stared him straight in the eyes. He had tears welling up at the corners, and his round cheeks turned redder.

"I'm sorry, brother. It's just with all the crazy news on TV, the attacks and fucked up weather, I…"

"The girl's a runaway from New York, and some assholes back at Moe's were planning on doing some bad things, man. I couldn't let that happen. You remember the psycho back at the village, with that girl?"

Jim nodded. "My Loc."

"Yeah, that's it. Same kind of shit, same kind of assholes. Brother." I let my eyes bore deep into his. I could feel him relax, and slowly his smile returned.

"I'm sorry, Jay. I am. I love ya, man, and I… I wor—" His face froze in a tormented expression of regret, anger, and sadness. His deep green eyes bulged.

That's when it all went to shit.

***

Jimbo's Drive-In Parking Lot.

Hector slowly walked toward the side steps of the diner, wiping the tears from his face, and stopped.

He heard something behind him. He tilted his head as the rain poured in cold, yellow sheets. The thunder drummed. Lightning danced all around him.

It was nothing, he told himself. But more than likely, it was overwhelming guilt that made him paranoid. He felt his chest tighten, and despite the cold temperatures, he found himself sweating like he was back in Mexico working the fields.

There it was again. He froze.

His pulse drummed in his temples. His heart pounded.

Was he drunk? Was it just the storm and the news on the radio that had him on the edge of a nervous breakdown? Every muscle in his body tensed, as the low, monotone sound grew louder.

From behind him. No, wait. All around him.

Cold sweat mixed with the freezing rain.

That's when he saw the figures coming out of the shadow of the storm. The two teen girls they'd killed were lumbering toward him. They were *dead*. His head swam. White flashes of lightning painted the area, and Hector could see every bloody detail.

"*Dios Madre*," he muttered in a whisper.

For the love of all that's holy, they *were* dead. He'd seen Isandro slit the girl's damn throat wide open and watched her bleed out. Now, she stood before him with jagged hunks of blood-encrusted flesh hanging loosely from her neck, her skin a ghostly white. Her eyes were black as pits, but somehow seemed to bore into him with a cold and burning darkness that made every part of his body ache.

"No, thi…this can't." He made the sign of the cross and tried to move. His legs failed him. Then, the dead girl's twin sister stepped out from the darkness and slowly walked toward him. He felt his blood freeze.

The rain poured down like frozen bullets from heaven. Each drop a painful assault on his exposed skin. He tried to break his stare on the dead twins as they trudged through the mud toward him, but all his body would allow were a few feeble steps backward.

"Who? Wha…" He tried to speak, but his words abandoned him. All he could do was stare deep into their black, sorrow-filled eyes.

They inched painfully closer. He couldn't move.

Lightning painted the parking lot.

He was aware of his surroundings, and his breath caught deep in his chest. His body was filled with horror as he looked around the parking lot.

Thunder rumbled like cannons above him, and he thought his heart would explode out of his quivering chest.

Before him, all around were over at least two-dozen shambling forms, all with the same awkward gait and letting out low moans.

As a volley of lightning lit the area, he panicked to see that beyond the diner's parking lot, sitting on a hill, was a cemetery. The mob of people was coming from there. "In God's name..." hector croaked. He shook his head, hoping it was the booze and the pot. Yeah, that was it, the weed must have been laced or some shit. Deep down, he knew he was wrong. Dead wrong. This was an act of God. An angry God. A vengeful God. It was the end times, and God was pissed. He began to cry.

They were dead. All of them. Fucking dead! He mouthed prayers as his tears matched the rain pelting his face.

He tried to move. He managed to get one foot to respond to his pleas. He spun and tried to run for the stairs, but slipped in the deep mud and fell. The twins were on him, and he stared up at the black night sky. No stars, just a darkness that offered nothing, save sporadic lightning flashes and cold rain. One of the twins obscured his rain-filled view of heaven, appearing above him. Her throat gaped open, exposing bloody skin, slit muscles, and arteries dangling on his face like cold spaghetti slathered in a frigid meat sauce.

She stared deep into his eyes. Like a dog tilting its head at a squeak toy, she looked at him. After a long terror-filled moment, she leaned down until she was a mere two inches from Hector's face. It wasn't the violent wound in her young neck that made him to weep even harder. No, it was her eyes.

"Forgive me," he mouthed to the girl and to God. He didn't flinch when the girl's teeth tore into his throat, and she fed.

He shook with white-hot pain. All over his body, many new sets of teeth dug and ripped at him, rending flesh from bone. He cried out into the pouring rain, but he was ready to die. He deserved it and prayed God would forgive him. He knew damn well He wouldn't. He felt a burning in his stomach and a flurry of action and moans around him.

He squeezed his eyes shut. He didn't want to see. His soul couldn't bear to see the girl's face. Her eyes.

In those eyes, Hector could see there would be no penance. No forgiveness from God.

Those dark eyes held more sorrow and horror in them.

Those black eyes cried black tears, and he could have sworn he heard the young dead girl whisper from her cold mouth,

I'm sorry,

Then Hector was hurled into darkness, and all he knew was the cold embrace of death.

30.

Gun Love
Inside Jimbo's Diner

It all happened at once. A thunderclap rocked the diner, a flurry of gunshots came from somewhere in front of me, A tirade of Spanish cussing, the sound of breaking glass, and then,a sharp pain burst through my left arm.

The first bullet shattered the whiskey bottle in my hand and stuck in the wall. The second one split the door's window behind me into a thousand shards. It was the third one that hurt like a sonuvabitch.

The bullet sent me sprawling backward. My head smashed into the pay phone, knocking the receiver off the cradle, and I collapsed in heap against the wall. Glass rained down on me. A stinging, burning filled my backside. I felt warm blood on the back of my pants and legs. The shards of the whiskey bottle jammed deep into my ass and thigh.

I looked up at Jimbo, his face still held the same look of shock. My breath caught in my chest as I saw a red dot on his grease-stained t-shirt bloom into a red explosion. Pieces of bone, flesh, and blood painted me and the wall behind. The phone above me rang as the bullet lodged itself in the bell of its metal casing.

The torrent of Spanish cussing filled my ears as Jimbo's frozen gaze fell upon me. Blood seeped from the wound in his broad chest. My mind was a storm of images, sounds, and terrors. What the hell was going on? Too much damn booze. I cursed my demons and myself.

"Jay…" Jimbo cried. And as if to answer him, a shot rang out. Jimbo's head jerked forward, bloody spit flew from his gaping mouth. A splattering of brain and bone shrapnel covered me. My pulse raced, my arm filled with red-hot pain, and my blood mixed with Jimbo's on the floor beneath me.

"Jimbo...." My breath gushed from my lungs when the full weight of the big man collapsed on top of me. I could feel the glass bore deeper into my leg. My arm screamed in pain, and I heard myself cry out. It was echoed with laughter. I knew that laugh.

Fuck me runnin'. I gritted my teeth, trying to bury the pain. My head was a cluster-fuck of shock, confusion, and rage. It raced with frenzied thoughts of Inez and Bellia, the shit-bag Governor, and my dead best friend, sprawled across my bleeding lap. There was no way in hell it could be that murderous asshole. He was sent to Oklahoma for twenty-five to fucking life.

"Hola, Ranger. Remember me?"

That voice. I didn't know the elevator to Hell went this goddamn low.

I swallowed hard and tasted copper. My gut rolled at the thought that it wasn't mine.

It was that shit-bag gang-banger Dianira. With my one good arm I hugged Jimbo, and I knew he was dead. A deep burning inside me began to grow. It wasn't the pain or the blood.

I kissed my friend on the side of his mangled head and whispered.

"Semper Fi, brother." I squeezed him with my good arm, and then wiped the gore from my eyes. I shifted the big man off just enough to allow me to reach my .45 on my right hip. I found it, popped loose the clasp on the holster and gripped the pistol.

Then my wrist erupted with bone-shaking pain.

I heard the scream of a young girl and some pretty damn foul words in Spanish.

Stacy Jo.

I smiled, and with my aching hand, snatched the pistol from the holster.

31.

Need Me

Stacy Jo heard the gunshots and instinctively slammed her back against the wall of the small bathroom. Screams of panic and shouts came through the flimsy door. The shouts were in Spanish, and whoever was speaking was pissed off.

Then she heard cold-hearted laughter. She could feel the burning hate through the hollow door. The scarred face of the creepy-ass Mexican that winked at her back in the booth flashed across her mind. She nodded.

"Motherfucker." Her teeth clinched in a sneer. She wasn't one to help cops, but this Ranger dude was cool. He'd given her a ride, food without any bullshit. She took a hit off of the bowl and held it. Releasing the smoke, she heard the chaos and had to do something.

Another round of shots rang through the dingy, tiled room. The room rocked, and thunder seemed to be punching through the paper-thin walls.

She flinched at the sound, her hand found the hilt of the Buck knife in her backpack. She ran to the door and slowly opened it a crack. She wished she'd left the door closed.

She could see one of Mexican guys hurrying to stand, while the other pulled a gun on the white kids in the booth right outside the bathrooms.

Beyond them, she winced and lost her breath as she caught the sight of the Ranger's cowboy boots underneath another pair of legs. Thick, grease stained sneakers laying soles up were attached to the motionless body.

Stacy Jo strained to look closer, and her chest tightened like a vise as she saw the pool of blood spreading out from the prone Ranger's location behind the booth.

A blinding flash of lightning whitewashed the young girl's tears as she stared out into the bloodbath of the diner. She needed to do something. She caught the Ranger's blood-covered boots moving. Kicking in the thick, coagulating fluid on the old floor. Her face broke into a trembling smile. The guy may have been a prick and a drunk, but he did help her. That's more than any adult had ever done in her seventeen years on this hellhole of a planet. She gripped her knife tighter, inhaled deeply, and then slowly let it out.

The closest asshole was a big dude, slowly walking toward the Ranger. Stacy Jo could see another figure coming at him from the right, a pistol in his hand. Cold sweat poured down her face and back. She felt like she was standing outside in the storm. She didn't have time to think about the weather.

She slammed the door open, it banged against the wall as she ran like a cat at the big Mexican. She heard more shouting. Screaming. It was her own frenzied voice that filled the diner. She leapt, landing with all her weight on his burly frame. The man grunted as she swung down with all her might, burying the knife to its hilt in the man's chest. Warm blood bathed her trembling hand as she clawed at the big man's eyes. From deep inside her, a feral, primal scream flowed out as she gouged and battered the big man. All sound was lost in loud barrage of thunder. It rocked the diner, and a flurry of lightning bathed all the inhabitants in a glowing light.

Then, in a ghastly whisper, the power went out. All went black.

32.

Thug

Sonuvabitch. The girl's scream signaled she was okay. I gripped the pistol, raising it up at the black figure coming straight at me in the darkness. It weighed heavy in my wet hand. I wasn't sure if it was blood or sweat, but that didn't make a damn difference. The lights going out was the best thing for me. At least now, this piece of shit and me were on the same playing field. Well, except for the bullet in my goddamn arm. I would kill for a shot of whiskey, but that wasn't going to happen anytime soon.

"Dianira, drop the fucking gun," I shouted into the blackness. The shape I assumed was the shit-bag gang-banger kept walking slowly toward me. Like he was savoring it. Asshole.

"Oh, senor McCutcheon. Did you miss me, esé? I really missed you." The voice was filled with daggers and thirst.

"Hell, dip-shit, you have enough time to miss me while you were making sweet man-love with your cellmate Bubba Bigprick? I bet you were the bottom." Although it killed me to do it, I shifted Jimbo's limp body to my left, using him as cover, while I rested my pistol arm on his broad shoulder.

"Ha. It's good to see you haven't lost your sense of humor, pendejo." His voice slowly pushed through the darkness. "After all, esé, don't they say that laughter is the best medicine?"

I couldn't see shit. A bright wash of light splintered the darkness, bathing the psychopath in a yellowish light. He was five feet away. A brutal grin split his battered face. My arm flared with pain, and I could feel the broken glass inch deeper into my thigh as Jimbo's body weight pressed down on me.

I had the piece of shit murderer in my sights. Lightning danced and flitted, providing the only light in the diner, casting demonic shadows on the old movie posters and road signs Jimbo had collected over the years. Dianira never took his deep-set, beady eyes off me. Bastard.

I pulled the trigger. The shot went wide, exploding a hanging light from the yellowing ceiling.

"Fuck!"

I could still hear the girl screaming and wrestling with the goon to my right. She needed me. Dianira snapped his head toward the commotion and didn't look happy. Good.

"Quit dancing with that bitch. We got shit t—" His words cut off as a dark form jumped the prick from behind. The man was short, stocky, and strong. *Whitney*. The old, tough-as-nails truck driver's name brought a wide smile across my face. It didn't last long as pain replaced it. I took the opportunity to try and get out from under Jimbo. My chest tightened, and I forced back a tear as I gently laid my best friend onto the cold, blood-covered floor. His blank eyes stared at me in a frozen plea for help.

The two wrestled in the darkness, save a few sporadic blasts of lightning. Whitney was one tough sonuvabitch He was a Navy Seal in 'Nam and strong as a damn ox. The old man knew his way around a barroom and was no stranger to blood. He was going to give me the time I needed to get this insane shit under control. So I thought.

A deafening gunshot blared through the diner, and as I got to my knees, my gut wrenched as *Whitney* slumped to the floor in a sick thump—his bearded face now a bloody wreck. A bullet hole split his mouth and nose. Shattered teeth, bits of skin, and shredded lips exploded in a red fountain into the cold, air.

I didn't have time to mourn for the trucker or Jimbo. I fired one at the Mexican prick, but the hours of booze were kicking my ass. I knew I couldn't hit the broad side of a barn even if I was on the goddamn inside.

"Fuck me!" I screamed, as the slide locked back on my pistol.

Okay, plan B, asshole. I only had a second to close in on this scumbag. I sprung from my crouch and closed the short distance faster than I thought my drunk legs could muster. The Mexican gang-banger turned toward me just as I drove my shoulder into his stomach. All air inside his wiry body rushed out in a loud *humph.* He fired a round from the pistol. I heard a girl scream and then the sound of shattering glass.

Stacy Jo!

Shit! No time.

We both went sprawling over the trucker's limp body. I heard the pistol clang to the floor and slide away. My left arm felt like three-dozen welders decided to build a damn skyscraper inside it. I still could take this shit-bag. I'd done it before.

I was on top of him. I threw my useless arm over his chest and sat up—trying to buy me enough time to get my legs underneath me. A fire raged in my arm as the guy grabbed the bleeding wound and squeezed. He cursed me in words I'd never even heard Inez's father say when talking about his daughter's worthless gringo of a fiancé.

Lightning offered flashes of vision—like a strobe light on fast-forward. The Thug squeezed harder on my arm, and I heard myself scream. The shit-bag laughed and squeezed harder. I didn't like that. I swung my pistol arm up toward his face, and the strobe light caught his 'oh shit' face, then the strobe went black again.

"Fuck you, pendejo." The thug grunted and punched with his other hand, knocking my gun aside as I squeezed the trigger. The bullet tore a hole into the linoleum close to his head. I heard the bitch let out a squeal.

The guy reacted fast. I used to be fast, but the hard years of fieldwork, booze, and self-loathing, had taken their toll on me. I felt a searing pain in my ribs. I thought I heard a crack.

The strobe was back. All I saw was the spinning ceiling fan as he twisted his hips and thrust his knees upward, sending me slamming into the booth to our left. The strobe went black again. This time, an eardrum shaking round of thunder took its place.

"Not this time, esé. Oh no. This time... I gut you like a pig. Just like your bitch ass friend." The thug's wide, blood slathered grin was above me. He looked like a Kodak film negative. I'd never seen so much anger and evil in one man's eyes. This sick fuck didn't just have to kill. No, he loved to kill. He had a taste for blood. I had to end him.

134

The strobe was replaced with darkness. I heard the piece of shit laughing. It chilled every inch of me. My arm flopped onto the floor. Shooting spasms of fire filled the damn thing. I could barely move. My body ached all over. I could still feel the blood running from the wound. My head was spinning, and the herky-jerky strobe light of lighting was making my gut rolled like a Maytag. I tried to twist my hips and legs to send the thug off balance, but he had his core weight centered over me.

"Pendejo." The thug leaned down, reached behind him, and pulled out a long, thin knife. The Strobe caught its glint then disappeared. I could feel his hot breath on my face. It smelled of pot, sex, and maple syrup. He laughed. I turned my face to avoid the fish and skunk smell. I felt the scumbag's lips against my cheek. I couldn't move underneath his dead weight. In the darkness, I still heard the sounds of a struggle back where the bathrooms were. My only hope that the kid was okay. I was in my own world of shit as I felt cold metal of the knife slowly cross my throat.

33.

Bad Girl

Stacy Jo spun around the big man's shoulders, facing him. She drove him backward, the pistol in his hand went off, and she heard the girl in the University of Houston t-shirt let out a horrid scream. A spray of blood painted the window behind her.

"Crazy bitch," the big man muttered, pawing at the knife buried in his burly chest. The guy fell, sending them both in a clumsy crash. Stacy Jo saw the smaller Mexican jumping up from the booth.

"Bobby," the guy's voice was shrill and filled with a panic. He danced around like his feet were on fire. Stacy Jo rolled against the counter and fought to catch her breath. Rain and thunder pounded the diner, and she could hear the Ranger and that vato fighting on the other side of the counter. Her heart felt as if it was going to implode in her chest, and her pulse raced like Tony Dorsett on speed. The big man lay in a pool of blood. His body twitched, and his thick legs kicked out. His meaty hands slapped at the Buck knife in his chest.

What the hell was going on? She frantically tried to wrap her racing mind around what was happening. No answers...no luck.

"What the hell you do, bitch?" the thin guy screamed at her, trying to help his big friend lying still on the floor. "Oh Christ, Bobby. Shit... shit... Fuck... shit," he cried out, falling over the man on the floor.

Stacy Jo lay on the floor and caught a glimpse of movement from the bathrooms. The chaotic flashes of lightning slowed the scene to a stop-motion cartoon like she and her best friend back in Arcadia Falls used to draw on the bottom of their notebook paper.

They'd draw a girl slowly, page-by-page, giving a guy a blowjob, and it'd be animated as they flipped each drawing. This was no drawing, and this guy in the blood stained Adidas jumpsuit staggering out of the darkness didn't look right. Blood and spit hung like a sling from his slack jaw. The man swayed back and forth. Spastic flashes of lightning broke up his drunken motions.

What Stacy Jo witnessed next seized every part of her. She tried to scream. She tried to warn the skinny guy trying to wake up the big guy lying in a spreading pool of blood. The guy in the jumpsuit lunged at the skinny guy, and the sound he made reminded her of the lions she'd watched on PBS, tearing into the zebras flesh. *Jumpsuit* lunged and bit the spastic dude, ripping a huge chunk of his flesh from his neck. The guy screamed out in agony and tried to fight off his attacker. It was too late. *Jumpsuit* was digging his teeth deep into his neck and shoulder. Blood and chunks of flesh tore from his thin frame.

"Dios Mio." Stacy Jo made the sign of the cross as she saw the big man...the dead man, slowly sit up. The knife still buried deep in his chest. Her mind fractured and every sense of reality splintered into a thousand horrid fragments. She backpedaled, only to find the coolness of the counter at her back to prohibit her retreat. Her head swirled, and she looked for an exit. The one by the pay-phone was clear.

She stood up. Her knees banged together, and her hands trembled. Her brown eyes shot open, and the big man slowly, awkwardly got to his feet. Her heart seized as behind him the college girl twitched, and then sunk her teeth into her boyfriend's face, ripping flesh and muscle from it. She swallowed.

Stacy Jo's stomach cinched tight, and she felt vomit rise in the back of her throat. The insanity of the moment froze her. Lightning cast the entire diner in surreal haze and thunder rumbled beneath her feet. She needed to get the hell out of Dodge. Now.

The big dead guy, College lovers, and the Adidas guy, all were slowly walking toward her. She needed to think. There wasn't a lot of time, and the chaotic storm wasn't making it any easier. She took a deep breath, saw the side door, and began to run for it. She skidded to a stop on broken glass and blood.

The Ranger, she thought and looked around. He was lying on the floor in a sea of blood with the scummy dude holding a knife to his throat.

Damn it! She had no idea what the hell was going on. People eating each other? The dead getting up, and with a hellfire case of the munchies? Her head raced, but there was no way she could leave the Ranger alone. Not after what he'd done for her. Hell, no. Reluctantly, she spun on her heal and saw a pistol lying in the floor next to some guy's leg. She picked it up and aimed it at the Mexican on top of the Ranger. She squeezed the trigger as a blast of white lightning lit up the scene. She didn't even look back as she jumped through the window of the diner. The glass shattered easy, having already weakened by gunshots. Stacy Jo felt a tidal-wave of jagged glass rip into her skin as she escaped into the raging storm.

Her scream was lost in the wash of thunder.

34.

Lowdown in the Street

I kicked up with my legs with all I the strength I had left. The prick on top of me let out a loud cry the same time a gun shot rang out from my right. I knew that sound. It was my pistol. But who?

The girl. Stacy Jo. She was still alive. Tough chick. I knew I liked her for a reason. I allowed myself a millisecond to grin and then took advantage of the opportunity.

I spun my hips, and it sent Dianira rolling off to the left, into the darkness. My arm still burned like a bitch, but I hoped to live long enough to pay his sorry-ass back. I staggered to my feet, and my head felt like my brain was inside a fishbowl. I inhaled slowly, let it out, and saw the shit-bag in the shadows grabbing at his shoulder. Good. The kid hadn't killed the asshole. It was my turn. I pulled the Ka-Bar from its sheath on my belt, smiled at the gang-banger, and took a step toward him. I heard her scream.

The supernatural storm raged on. The wind and rain rocked and brutally attacked the diner. The frantic lighting continued to cast jumping images in my pain and booze filled head. I froze. I couldn't believe what the hell I was seeing.

"Stac…" the words caught like nails in my throat as I watched her leap out the window. The fat guy, who had a big Buck knife sticking out of his chest, was ripping skin, muscle and fat from one of the college kid's face. They looked at me for help as blood poured from their cheeks and necks like a fire hydrant in the summer time. Her large blue eyes fixed on me. My chest again began to pound.

"No," my words were lost in the swirling storm. I wanted to help. My pistol clanked to the floor, she disappeared beneath the thrashing arms and bloody hungry maws of the two monsters.

I reached out and pulled them off, but only made it two steps before a sharp burning sensation filled my back. I cried out, as the all too familiar pain of a knife pierced my lower back. Guessing by how it suddenly became a bitch to breathe, my right lung was toast.

"Your ass is mine, pendejo. I will make you suffer. Suffer like I did." Dianira lifted me up with the blade of his knife, and my legs felt like I was walking in Jell-O. He shoved me toward the side door. We passed the feeding frenzy. I felt my stomach churn and my heart ache as I heard the girl crying for help beneath the pile of death and gore. He snatched me by the belt and the knife handle, throwing me through the glass side door.

What the hell was this guy? A Mexican super villain? The bastard wasn't at all affected by all the fucking zombies munching on the living. What the hell?

Hundreds of shards of glass bore into my skin as I flew out into the freezing rain. I felt my body hit something solid, a person maybe. I didn't have a hell of a lot of time to analyze as I slammed into the mud of the parking lot.

The world was a hellacious blur. The storm raged on. Thunder rumbled the ground like a battalion of tanks were running the diner over. Lightning flashed like a goddamn Iron Maiden concert, and the rain pounded down like frozen nails from the black sky. My mind was a damn jigsaw puzzle on a keg of Jameson. The fucked up weather. Those jack holes eating people. What the hell? I had far more worse shit to worry about as my eyes went from blurry to clear, just in time to see that shit-bag Dianira standing over me with a pistol.

Fuck me.

35.

Sleep Warm.

Sharp, needle-like raindrops felt good against her skin. Stacy Jo was grateful for the thick mud she landed in next to the dumpster. She didn't have much time to relax. The entire parking lot of the diner was slowly being swallowed up by staggering forms. The teen was all too aware of what those nasty bastards were there for.

She could still hear the sound of fighting inside the diner, but she had to get away. Her heart weighed heavy leaving the Ranger, but there was nothing she could do for him now. She waited and finally a spot opened up. She ran toward the Ranger's car. If all else failed, the vehicle offered at least some form of protection.

The rain pelted down like an angry God as she forced her way through the groping and grabbing undead. Finally, she reached the passenger's side door and yanked it open, jumped inside, and slammed the door.

She waited.

Nothing came. The moaning, sorrow-filled cries of the undead filled the parking lot, but nothing attacked the car. She crossed herself—an old habit form her Catholic days. Something she hadn't done in a very long time. Hard rain pounded the car, sounding like mini-cannons going off in a taunting-syncopated pattern.

She lay there, on the floorboard of the car, hoping for a miracle.

36.

It's so Hard.

"Hola, puta. I told ya, your ass was mine." Dianira smiled wide. In the flashes of light, he looked like a demon. Rain pelted my eyes, and I frantically wiped it away so I could see. I tried to move, but he had one booted foot on my chest. Pushing the knife in my back deeper inside me. I heard things snap and pop and fought to inhale. It wasn't looking good for this hombre, and all I could think of was my loves. Inez and baby Bellia back home…Houston.

I hadn't really prayed in a long time. The half-assed attempt earlier proved it was a damned fool's errand. Too late to start now. No deathbed conversions for this old warhorse. I looked up defiantly at the piece of shit gang-banger and spit at him.

Dianira laughed, letting the harsh rain wash the spit away.

"Oh, you do have some *cajones* after all. It wasn't just the badge that gave you the big dick after all, huh, Ranger?" He knelt down on my chest. I felt a searing pain jolt my body from head to toe as his smile never faded.

"Go fu—" My breath left me and white burning pain took its place. It only made the asshole smile wider. Behind him, the black sky danced with forks of lightning that held tinges of red and yellow. It reminded me of pus, of rot and death. Fitting. I coughed and felt blood spray from my wrecked lung and saw it splatter his grinning face.

"I'll taste your blood, pig. I will drink it. Because of you, I sat rotting in that 4x6 cement shit-box. Because of you, I lost my wife and son, bitch. All because you couldn't just take the fucking deal and walk away, I missed the death of my Mamma." He used the back of his wrist to wipe the tears way, but never let his cold brown eyes lose focus on me.

"No, esé." He used his off hand to go through my jacket pockets. He stopped suddenly as a new barrage of thunder and lightning kicked the hell out of the night sky. I could sense others gathering closer, but I could feel the shock starting to kick in. It wouldn't be too long.

He sat down on my thighs and pulled out my badge wallet. "Oh, what do we have here?" He flipped the leather open with the barrel of my gun. "Oh, I'm gonna take this as a keep sake, if ya don't mind, Officer." It wasn't a question. He ripped the Texas Ranger Star out of the wallet and shoved it into his soaking wet shirt.

The shadows around us seemed to creep in. Slowly. My head hurt. Not as bad as the stabbing pain in my back, but I couldn't be sure if it was the lightning or the whitewash of shock finally kicking in. Either way. I cried. I'd never see Inez again. I'd never see my lovely Bellia grow up.

"Let's see what we have here?" he mocked. Checking my other pockets, he let out a deep laugh and pulled out the keys to the 'Cuda.

My gut wrenched as I watched through rain and tear drenched eyes, as the piece of shit killer pulled out my wallet and found photos of my wife and baby. Then slowly, my I.D. with my address on it.

"Well, well, Ranger. Wow. She is one hot piece of ass." Dianira shot me a wink and dug the barrel of the gun into my chest. "Ohhheee, son. I could eat that all day.?" He let out a laugh that echoed out into the hell-storm.

"Plea..." It was all I could muster. I could feel my blood running out into the mud of the parking lot. I tried to scream. Tried to swing at the dick-bag. Nothing responded. I was dead. Not yet, but goddamn close.

"Oh, I'm gonna *'please,'* is alright. Trust me. I am going to do things to her body that you've never dreamed." He licked his lips, staring at the photo. "Esé, before I'm done, this bitch is going to know a real man fucked her. Hell, yes." He turned his lecherous gaze to me. His expression melted into one of stone cold hatred and determination.

He shoved the photo into his pocket and leaned in close.

"When I'm done with her, Ranger, I'm going to gut her like a pig, and then," his mouth slowly spread into the most evil smile I'd ever seen. He continued. "I am going to slice your little girl's head off. Then, you will truly know what it's like to have lost everything." He stared at me for a long moment. Our eyes locked. Matched hate for hate.

I looked around. Those shadows weren't just darkness of the storm, no, they were other dead fucks walking and reaching out for chow. Sweet Jesus. What hell was going on here? I knew no brilliant answers were coming, I just prayed for my girls. I knew my role in this horrific play was over. I fucked up one last and fatal time. All I could hope for, was Inez would take the baby and run for Mexico. My luck was never that good.

"Hum, looks like it's time to visit..." Dianira read my I.D., "215 Hudson Street, Houston, Texas. Oh, and I made damn sure you'll live long enough to be a Big Mac meal for these... *infierno desovar.*" He smiled, stood up, and spit on my face. He gave the keys a playful jingle and kicked me in the ribs a few thousand times. His laughter ruled the parking lot filled with death and yellow rain.

It might have been mercy from some god up there, but I was numb, no pain. I did see dark shadows erupt into a mob. A mob of rotting, staggering forms. All in different states of rot and decay. All were dead.

I felt the cold rain batter my face. My vision became a black and white montage of images. I watched the clumsy forms fall out the diner. One by one, they all staggered down the steps, and into the mud slogged parking lot. The kid from New York was nowhere to be seen. I struggled to move. Every part of my body pulsed with pain and rage. The growing mob slowly made its way toward me.

It was over. My greatest and final fuck up. I felt my shoulders sag and my guts rolled. Then came a heavy sadness. As if every sin I'd laid bare on this world was coming home to roost on my soul. And, it demanded retribution. Every shit-bag criminal that drew on me and I had to put a bullet into. Every time I'd gotten drunk and got into a barroom brawl and kicked the shit out of some guy. Every time I slept with a drunk barfly and left her lying naked in some fleabag motel. Then there was Inez. The damage I'd done to her. The love of my life. I felt tears welling up in the corners of my blind eyes.

I heard the pounding of thunder and another sound that reminded me of how my dad, drunk off his ass, would sit at the dinner table and suck the marrow from the chicken bones and proudly proclaim, 'Hell boy, that's the best part.' Then he'd backhand me. I hated that man.

The cold, brutal images quickly flashed through my rattled brain. The sounds of those undead things grabbed at me. I cautiously opened my eyelids. I wished to hell I didn't.

I watched the red taillights of a Cadillac speed off into the storm as I fought to get to my feet. The throng of dead were getting closer, surrounding me. Despite the darkness, I still prayed for my girls, and kicked one—a burly kid, who looked to be a high school or college aged footballer. My boots found his balls, and he sprawled backward, toppling over two or three others. The storm raged on, and I closed my eyes—the agonizing pain of broken bones, cuts, and contusions wracked my shaking body. Knowing that I'd failed them once again, I cursed myself and wished for one last shot of whiskey.

I looked around the muddy parking lot, the staggering and crawling bodies surrounded me. Dead fucking bodies. They were all in different stages of rot and decay. The sadness filled me. Surrounded me like a stake through the heart. I slowly got to my feet. It hurt, muscle and bone rubbed together like nails against rusty screws. My head spun and dark images of the Mexican gangbanger, Stacy Jo, Whitney the trucker, Jimbo, Robbie... The images tore at me, and I cried...

I could feel my surrender. My giving up.

I stood there in the yellowish colored mud and wept. A brilliant flash of lightning washed the entire parking lot.

Then I saw it. Lying there in the soggy mush. A photograph. Half of it at least. I fought off a guy in a Houston Astros jersey, bent down, and pulled it from the mud. I stood and stared at the image on wet photo.

More tears flowed and mixed with rain as it splattered on the photo. It was of Inez and me on the day Bellia was born. I was smiling. I felt even colder, if that was possible.

"Inez and Bellia McCutcheon, I love you," I managed to shout into the freezing storm as the dead crowd surrounded me. I flailed my tired arms in every direction. They struck something. I could feel my knuckles sting as they hit bone. It didn't seem to stop those dead bastards from coming.

Above me the sky was pitch black, save the darting veins of lightning that crisscrossed and lit up the parking lot. When Dianira stomped my ass and shanked me, left me for dead, I figured I'd wake up in Hell with Satan's flames roasting my ass. This was worse. A hell of a lot worse. My chest and side were soaking wet. Not from the rain, and as I pulled my hand away, it wasn't all blood either. I staggered back, keeping the dead at bay. I stared at my hand and laughed. My laughter sounded like I was in a huge canyon—echoing and cold. The sweet smell of whiskey filled my nostrils as I looked at my hand again.

"Dumb-ass," I said, and took out the flask with a gapping blade hole in its center. Only the tip had cut my skin. Laughter called again from my body.

A women got too close and grabbed my arm. I grabbed her hand and shirt; trying to shove her away. She leaned down and our gazes locked. She bared her bloodstained teeth. I could see bits of meat and arteries packed in them. I fought to breathe, and then she thrust down and tried to make a midnight snack out of my throat.

No. I heard a voice burning like a four alarm blaze in my gut. *Suck it up, bitch.* There ain't no sad, martyr shit going down tonight. My own thoughts raced through me like a command. It sounds like some kind of hippie-dippie bullshit, but it's true.

I almost shat my dungarees, as I raised my head and saw the thick horde of moaning and groaning zombies looking at me like I was goddamn T-bone. My gaze fell to the rainy ground, and there I saw it—all I needed to keep my moving. To keep me fighting. In the muddy dirt was the photo of my girls. I knelt as fast as my broken body would let me, snatched it up, and shoved it into my pocket.

I took a deep breath and readied myself. My girls ain't dying tonight.

Neither am I.

37.

Hi-Fi- Mama.

Loud pings of hail and rolling thunder shook the 'Cuda. Stacy Jo lie curled up on the floor, waiting for the dead to go away. She cringed as she heard the Mexican's evil laughter and the groans of the Ranger, from somewhere out in the parking lot.

Her heart raced, and breathing became difficult. Getting baked was the only thing that kept her panic attacks at bay. No way in hell could she spark up now. Her body twitched with fear and uncontrollable anxiety.

A thunderclap rocked the car and almost causing her to puke. The moans of the dead and laughter only escalated her panic. In a flash, she remembered the Ranger's gun in the glove box. The small knob opened the box, and she snatched the gun, a glint of chrome caught her eye. A breath of relief escaped her nerved-racked body.

Car keys. She grinned.

Within seconds, she had the key in the ignition, and she prayed she wasn't too late. The Ranger was the first guy that was kind to her. He saved her when he had no worry or business to. She owed him.

With a quick twist of her thin wrist, the big block engine roared to life. All the zombies turned their blood-covered faces toward her.

Just what she wanted.

She yanked the lever into reverse, punched the gas pedal, and then jammed it into drive and cranked the wheel.

There was a Texas Ranger to save.

38.

Mexican Blackbird
The McCutcheon House
215 Hudson Street
Houston, Texas
1:30 a.m.

Inez stared at the storm through the large bay window. She had a clear view of the road from their house at the middle of the cul-de-sac. Thick raindrops assailed the glass. They sounded like bullets in the silence of the split-level ranch. The Television was on mute behind her. It offered a soft glow, but she couldn't bear to listen to any more news of the storm and the terrorist attacks. Lightning danced and flashed, making her jump with each frenzied strike. She'd been on edge since Jay's first call.

She had laid Bellia down hours before, but couldn't sleep. She never could when Jay wasn't home. There'd been too many of these nights over the course of the past year. She sipped absently from the Diet Coke and waited.

She had spent the last four years waiting. She knew what she was getting into when she started dating the Texas Ranger. But she never had any clue to just how many demons her fiancé had. He was the angriest man she'd ever known. He'd never laid a hand on her or the baby, and she knew in her heart he didn't have it in him. It was other people she worried about. Then there was the drinking. He'd always enjoyed a cold beer after work, and maybe a little more with his buddies on the weekends, but it had gotten worse when they split up a year ago. She could live with the booze. It was the infidelity she couldn't handle. There'd only been two incidences since they'd been together, but Inez had her own demons. Trust was her biggest. All that aside, she still loved him more than any other man she'd ever known. His heart was as big as the state of Texas, and his intentions were always good. She smiled soberly at that thought and the memory of how her Mama used to always tell her, 'The road to hell was paved with good intentions.'

"You were always so right, Mamma," she whispered, her breath fogging the glass. She didn't know what to do. She had given him ultimatums after ultimatums. He'd tried, but always seemed to find a way to sabotage himself. When she talked to her Papi on the phone early that evening, he'd told her to pack up the baby and come home. Part of her wanted too. After all, how many chances did Jay deserve? Sure they were in love. Sure they were engaged, but his career in the Rangers was his passion and his last anchor to sanity. Besides her and Bellia, she hoped.

"Damn it!" She crinkled the can and bit her lip. *Now he even has me putting us in second place behind his damn job.* She saw her sad reflection shaking her head in the window. Inez walked to the kitchen and tossed the ruined soda can into the garbage. She opened the refrigerator, took another soda out, and closed the door. She cracked it open and sipped. The images on the door caught her breath.

A myriad of images plastered the Frigidaire. Memories that made her instantly smile. A photo of her and Jay on their first date—a ZZ Top concert that she hated—but Jay wanted to go. He was so hot she couldn't say no. Another photo of Jay holding Bellia the day she was born. That was the first time in a long while; she'd seen him truly beaming with happiness. Hot tears stream down her cheeks. She went from one memory to the next and the tears fell more intense with each one.She knew damn well what she wanted, needed to do.She loved the grumpy bastard, despite all his issues. They'd find a way to make it. He'd come home; they'd weather this storm out both outside and in.

"Damn you, Ranger. I love you, you loco sonuvabitch." She found herself giggling and crying, that made her miss him more. She looked up at the clock on the wall and time seemed to be crawling backward. She leaned against the fridge and sipped from the soda. Her heart skipped a beat as she heard the low roar of a car's exhaust pulling in front of the house. muscle car. Then headlights broke through the darkness of the dining room. She found herself smiling, and a sharp sob caught in her chest.

"Jay!" she shouted. She tossed the can into the sink and ran to the front door.

The car's engine shut off by the time she got to the door, she unlocked it, and whipped it open with an unabashed excitement. She and Bellia needed their Ranger home, and here he was. She was still crying as the door hit the wall, and her heart dropped out of her chest.

"Hola, mamacita. It's not fit for man, nor beast out there." The lanky stranger smiled wide, holding a badge, and then lean against the door jamb.

Lightning and thunder lit the night behind him, encasing him in a dark shadow that made Inez's skin freeze and crawl. She back peddled until she fell onto the stairs.

"Have no fear, my dear. Always trust your car to the man with a star." The stranger stepped inside, slammed the door, and locked it.

Bellia began crying from upstairs. The stranger tossed the car keys on the floor, gazed upstairs with wild eyes, and licked his thick lips.

"Oh, good. My second course is awake. But first, puta, I have a message from your dead pendejo." His smile seemed more wide than humanly possible as he pulled out a badge from his jacket.

Inez's tears poured down, and fear overtook her as she tried to crab walk up the stairs.

Jay's badge. She screamed.

Baby Bellia matched her terror. The storm wailed and battered the outside of the McCutcheon home. Hiding the horrific events that were now tearing apart and scarring the inside.

39.

I Got the Message.
The parking lot of Jimbo's Rusty Cactus Diner
1:40 a.m.

A zombie bitch in a *Flock of Seagulls* t-shirt tilted her head like a stray dog hearing a screeching tire for the first time. Except, this time, it truly was tires squealing, and the mighty roar of a 426 Hemi I recognized all too well.

The sky was jet black and spewed piercing ice pellets that struck my exposed skin like thousands of small daggers. I let out a wheezy laugh, as it seemed that God himself was pissing on me. Telling me, my luck had done run out.

Screw that. I'll decide when my ticket gets punched. Not today.

The smell of the dead hung in the heavy air like a low-laying cloud and, I coughed the vile shit from my burning lungs. I managed to get my back against the side of a Chevy pick-up. I knew it wasn't the smartest move in the world, but defending what's in front of me is a hell of a lot easier than having to worry about my six.

A flurry of rotting arms grabbed at me. A wave of snapping teeth bite the cold air, too damn close for my liking. I kicked and punched with whatever energy I had left. This old jarhead wasn't going down easily.

I fought until my body would respond. The zombies tore, pulled, and yanked me back down. The roar of the engine obliterated the pounding rain and cries of the dead.

The horde split like a well-place bowling ball. No 9-10 split here. Now, the car made a clean strike out of all those undead bastards. I heard myself laughing again and balled my hands into bloodied fists.

It was the girl. I smiled. Actually fucking smiled. Hell, it was the first good turn I'd have in the past twenty-four hours. I was going to take it.

The 'Cuda slid in a half circle and came to a stop. I could smell the brakes mix with the foul air and dead. I had only a small window to act.

A number of arms and hands latched onto me and dragged me back, spinning me around. Fierce snarls and guttural moans filled my ears. I managed to catch my balance and fend off a short guy in mechanic's overalls. I dislocated his jaw; sending him falling into the crowd.

The dirt was quickly turning to mud, and my boots began to sink into the muck. Stacy Jo's shouts were lost in the raging storm and the groaning of the clamoring undead.

The car wasn't far. I kicked out and caught what looked like a naked dead teenager in the stomach. Her throat was sliced wide open—a fresh wound. It didn't take Sherlock fucking Holmes to figure out what scumbag did that. She fell to the mud and started to get back up.

"Ranger, come on!" Stacy Jo screamed.

I looked, and she had opened the passenger side door. It lay wide open, and if I didn't get my sorry ass there quick like, then one or more of the flesh-eating sonuvabitches would be on her like flies on a cow patty.

I turned and ran toward the car. Stacy Jo was smiling. I could see her look of overwhelming fear, rage . Damn, I knew that look all too well. I was a mere five feet from the 'Cuda's door when I fell.

Stacy Jo screamed as I rolled over and saw a long, puffy-haired guy wearing a mud covered WASP baseball jersey. Right then I should have been fearing for my life. Worried about my family, even Stacy Jo; but, hell no. The only thing that raced through my mind was, *What the hell is a WASP and why does it have a codpiece with a saw blade stuck through it?* It's strange what your mind does in times of deep horror.

My millisecond detour was derailed by a deafening gunshot—just above my head. The metal-head's right eye disappeared in a red spray of blood, bone, and brain juice. His slack body flopped onto my legs.

Stacy Jo continued firing as I kicked the dead guy off me, fighting off the hungry hands and bloody maws.

I finally got free and jumped into the car; more like fell in a sloppy heap into the car.

"Close the damn door!" Stacy Jo ordered, as she jumped into the seat and slammed her door.

A cluster-fuck of hands grabbed at me and the door, but those rotting bastards didn't get the chance to dine on this Ranger; hell no. The 'Cuda surged forward as the runaway from New York stomped down, putting the pedal to the metal. The nearly 3,000 pound muscle car fish-tailed sending a spray of mud and bodies flying into the muck of Jimbo's Diner's parking lot. That thought created a catch in my chest. All the death. No time for that, Marine. Adapt and overcome. I kept telling myself that, and someday, maybe today, that shit will run ashore.

"You okay, old man?" Stacy Jo asked, driving into the storm.

"Yeah. Right as fuckin' rain, kid," I said, pulling myself up in the seat. "Of course, you know, you'll be pulling over as soon as we're clear of hell's half acre back there. Nobody drives *Alice,* but me."

She smiled and laughed. "Alice, huh?"

"Don't," was all I said.

I turned and looked out into the blackness of the storm—my heart burned and thoughts raced.

I was going to play this game out and save my family. The hell with the rest of the insane bullshit. I forced my legs to work and headed down the road. I had miles to go and an asshole to kill. I just hoped I made it there it time.

If this nightmare was real and it was the end of the world, then so be it. Not even the apocalypse could stop me. Before sunrise, I would kill Isandro, hold my wife and baby girl in my arms, and never leave them alone again.

My girls needed me, and I needed them. And even a parking lot filled with dead walkers wouldn't stop me. I was going back to Houston.

I tucked the photo into my blood-covered jacket and headed west.

I had to take care of one last thing.

Save my family and...

Kill me one fucking Mexican.

40.

Going Back to Houston.
Route 45 South
3:45 a.m.

We switched a few miles down the road, and Stacy Jo gave me an unexpected hug. I thought I'd heard her crying, but she did a damn good job of hiding it. I hugged her tightly and not a word was spoken. I knew we'd get through all this weird shit. Whatever this *shit* was. We got back in *Alice* and drove on—staring straight into the blackness.

The swirling and raging storm was a constant companion as the girl and I drove west. I wasn't sure if the walking dead followed us from the diner. I didn't give a damn. But there were a shit-ton of them lining the road as we drove.

My body felt like a flesh tube filled with cement and hand grenades. Moving any part took all the energy I could muster and hurt like hell. Pain oozed from every pore. My mind did jumping jacks trying to figure out what the hell had happened. How the fuck could have things gone so far south of shit that it made being dead look like a nice Sunday picnic in the park?

The rain was relentless and pounded the car as it separated the night from the shadows.

My mind flashed with gut-wrenching images of what that sonuvabitch Dinaria was doing to Inez and baby Bellia. I cursed myself again. I should have killed that bastard when I had the chance a long time ago. It was too late now. I might as well wish in one hand and piss in the other for all good it did me. The vile visions played inside my frozen mind as I drove toward home.

"How close are we?" Stacy Jo asked; for the first time, timidly. The voice sounded uncomfortable on her.

"Close. But not close enough."

"Ya think that asshole is there?"

I could tell she didn't want to ask the question.

I let her question float in the thick air. Man, I needed a damn drink.

She didn't ask again.

The rain and number of lumbering dead increased in mass the closer we got to Houston. It was a forty-five minute drive from Jimbo's Diner to my house. I sure as hell hoped that with all this supernatural, Twilight Zone shit that was swirling around, that we could magically warp me home. No such luck.

The sign read:

Houston ......10 Miles.

The furnace rumbled, and I trooped on.

The dead swelled the road all around us. And the storm of the apocalypse escorted us rest of the way.

41.

Dust my Broom
The McCutcheon Home
5:47 a.m.

The soft glow of sunrise was just starting to seep into the sky. Rain still punished the earth, while lightning and thunder slowly gave way to an eerie silence. We crested the hill and looked down on the housing complex where my house was.

The big sign that was usually well lit was bathed in darkness. It read: '*Azure Heights.*' The memory of fighting with Inez about buying a house in this stuffy, hoity-toity neighborhood wasn't my idea. She never had a real house and a real family. She wanted this, and I was more than happy to give it to her.

I stopped the car and gazed down on the gated community. It looked more like a cold, dark prison than a happy, '*let's go play golf with Biff and Buffy,*' white-collar development. There were several bodies walking around the complex.Random, terror-filled screams filled the cold night air. And sirens and alarms wailed off in the distance.

My gut roiled, and a biting acid filled my mouth. The whole knowing and not knowing thing felt like a punch in the balls. I need to get home.

I began down the hill and could see my house at the center of the cul-de-sac. The furnace of rage in my gut blasted with dire heat. It got a hell of a lot hotter the closer we drove. I stopped as I saw the Caddy parked at an angle in front of our house. The driver's side door left open. I could hear the Allman Brothers, "*In the Memory of Elizabeth Reed,*" blaring from the stereo. The furnace was stoked.

The cries of the dead or dying filled the cul-de-sac as I stepped stiffly onto the sidewalk in front of my house. The house was covered in darkness. The front door was wide open.

I parked the car and got out. Stacy Jo started to get out the other side. I motioned for the girl to stay in.

Stacy Jo leaned to see. "Ranger, I don't think you sh—"

"I have to, kid." I heard my words, and the coldness even scared me.

She grabbed my arm. I stopped and looked back at her. I could see her tears mix with the drying blood on her young face— creating a sick, clown-like make-up that made my stomach churn. I should never have picked her up. She might have actually have lived through this shit-pool. Her chances now were close to goddamn null.

I knelt down and took a breath. The smell and moans of the dead growing closer.

"You stay here. It's safer inside the car." I forced a smile. We both knew it was for shit. "Check the glove box, there should be more shells for the pistol." I stood up, and leaned back in. "Don't worry, if I need your help, you'll know right quick." I shot her a wink. "If all goes to shit, you climb your ass in the driver's seat, and you best get hell bent for leather out of here. Got me?"

She started to slide over into the driver's seat, nodding.

I nodded and slowly headed for the front door of my house.

The girl didn't want me to go. Hell, I didn't want to either— that would mean I had an answer to the darkest fears I'd had since I left Jimbo's. Some questions just aren't worth knowing the answers to. I felt a weak smile slip from my bloody face.

The air was thick with the smell of burning wood and rotting meat. The odd colored steam rolled off the blacktop. My well-worn, gore-caked cowboy boots sloshed through the puddles as I stopped and looked at my, our home.

I crossed the sidewalk, calling out Inez's name. As I crossed the blood-soaked threshold, I felt razor-sharp shivers cut at my bones. I sounded frail and thin.

'Now's not the time to go tits-up boy,' my father's gruff voice grated in my head like a chainsaw to my balls. I tucked it all away and checked my pistol—loaded and ready.

I stared into the darkness of the living room and waited. Not a fucking sound came back, except mocking silence.

Our house was swallowed in darkness. My feet slapped on the wet carpet. With the door open, the rain must have soaked it through. I looked down and saw that it wasn't rainwater on the beige carpet. It was red. *Blood.*

I turned and looked at the door. A big bloody smear covered the numbers. One hand print was clear on the white door. It was a small hand.

Inez, I cried out, or at least tried to. Fear had stolen my voice. I felt hot tears pour down my face and the furnace in my gut rage.

I stared down at the swirling mixture and caught the blood trail leading into the darkness, toward the hallway. I followed.

I heard the sound of sloshing behind me and I freeze. I swung with my pistol raised.

It was Stacy Jo. Her thin hands held up in a shaky surrender. I let out a deep breath and offered my hands up in return. I got it. She didn't want to be alone. I got that. I motioned for her to stay. She held my backup piece in her hand and leaned against the door jam. She didn't move—just watched me.

"Be careful," Stacy Jo whispered.

If I was a scared as she sounded, I was fucked.

I nodded at her and continued on, following the blood trail. A machine gun of thunder and its cruel sister lightning washed through the windows, casting the hallway in a sickly yellow haze.

Down the hallway, the bathroom door stood open. Next, the guest bedroom, and at the end, my den.

The trail led off in two directions. One went deeper forward into the house, toward the dining room. The other, left, toward the den. I could make out a faint glow coming from den, so I headed that way.

The once sweet smell of a cigar wafted into the hallway. My stomach to roll. The glow lit up the wall opposite the den, illuminating photos of Inez, Bellia, and me in happier times. My tears continued while the furnace blazed.

I rounded the doorway and looked inside. What I saw proved to me that no God existed, and if he or she fucking did, they were a soulless, spiteful bitch.

Inez lay on the leather couch, covered in blood. My Ranger badge buried deep into her forehead. Her skin, white as wax, and her beautiful, mahogany brown eyes stared blankly at the ceiling. Her chest was slit wide open. Her chest an empty cavity as flaps of roughly hewn skin and muscle laid loosely against her ribcage. Her heart lay on the carpet, like an empty fucking beer can.

I stared. Paralyzed. The tears came in torrents, and the furnace was about to blow. Every inch of my body and soul were set ablaze with a rage. A deep, prehistoric, violent rage I'd never felt before.

A shrill cry shook me from my hate-filled trance.

That's when I saw him. That sorry, sick son-of-a-bitch!

Isandro Dianira stood shirtless with his back to me. The glow came from a cigar held tightly in his mouth.

"Hola, puta." He was covered in blood from the greasy top of his head to the mud and gore covered soles of his prison-issued sneakers. The bag of shit slowly turned, and his smiled.The furnace in my aching gut ,was about bursting at its seams.

"You're fuckin' dead. You know that, don't ya." It wasn't a question, and he knew it. I started to bring the gun up, stepping forward, and froze.

I almost collapsed when I saw what the fucking monster held in his hands.

"Say hola, papa'." He squeezed Baby Bellia to his chest. His cold eyes never leaving me. He stroked my baby's cheek with the knife.

"I'll fucking gut you." I growled and stepped forward.

"Nah, uh. I am fuckin' impressed, Ranger. You don't look so good, esé. I thought bullets in your chest would have killed your punk ass." Isandro continued to trace Bellia's shrieking face.

"See, I told you, pendejo. With every long night I spent in that hellhole. With every bite I took of the shit they called food, I thought of you. I swore that I'd make you suffer. I am nothing if not a man of my word." His wide eyes turned from a dark brown to a blazing red, as if from the fiery pits of Hell itself. The fucking gang banger's grin snapped to a foul grimace, and he made a quick motion with the blade.

It all came down to this one horrific, nightmare second.

That sick fuck's insane laughter and wide bestial smile tore at my soul.

The furnace was a blast of fury, and all was lost.

I lunged forward, causing Dianira's blade to miss my baby girl. She fell out of his arms onto the blood-drenched carpet. I tried to catch her. Other hands suddenly reached out and caught my girl in midair.

A blur flashed into the room and too fast for me to see details..

It took a few seconds for my racing brain to put the images to some kind of reasonable thought. It was Stacy Jo. The girl pulled Bellia to her chest and raced toward the doorway.

No time to question anything. I grappled the gang-banger, and we crashed into my gun cabinet—shattering glass and splintering wood.

I landed on top of him. He swung the knife, but this time, I chopped down with a knife hand strike, sending the blade spinning across the room. I smiled and spit in his face. Now, the asshole was scared.

The furnace was finally free. I felt as though I left my battered body and rose above the horror flick below me. I watched *me* move in a savage ecstasy. My hands tore at his tattooed throat. The furnace demanded more and more blood. The rage consumed me. Ate me alive. I choked the shit-bag. The hunger filled me like the fire in my gut. As I heard the terrified cries of baby Bellia, I knew that while God may be a spiteful asshole, sometimes, just sometimes, Karma was a bigger bitch.

I let the furnace rule and the hunger take me. I fed it. My hands and arms ached and burned, but I didn't let go. He frantically bashed at my face and arms, but I was numb. His dark eyes bulged, his light brown skin turned a sickly shade of red, and then purple, as blood poured out his nose. I heard cold, animalistic laughter.

It was mine.

Dinaria let out a sickly gurgle as I squeezed harder. No death was good enough for this piece of shit. If I'd killed him a million times and it would never be good enough.

I stared into his unmoving—dead eyes.

I didn't let go of his throat.

Sitting there, I could hear the rain battering the house—our house.

I would have to be satisfied knowing that, in the end, the gutless, so-called bad-ass thug, screamed like the punk bitch I knew he always was.

The drumming of rain and pounding thunder surrounded me. I was lost.

Lost in the empty satisfaction of killing Dinaria.

Lost, knowing that Inez was gone.

Lost.

"Ranger..."

I heard Stacy Jo's voice.

Then I heard the sound of a baby crying.

I slowly got to my feet. Every bone, every inch of my flesh burned as if on fire. I didn't care.

42.

Softly to the Sun

The yellowish-red glow of sunrise filled the living room as we sat on the couch, watching it out of the bay window of our home. I held Inez tightly in my arms. Her limp, cold body weighed heavy as we sat and witnessed the day after the apocalypse begin.

She was dead. But her body, and her deep, loving brown eyes stared up at me. Those beautiful, enrapturing eyes. I had no idea how long I sat there. I could hear Bellia screaming in the other room, and Stacy Jo trying to calm her...It... It was a nightmare I just couldn't face. I slowly traced the soft curve of Inez's cheek, watching as my tears splashed on her cold, pale skin, rolling down.

"Tú eres el amor de mi vida, mi amor," I heard my soft words roll, as I caressed her face. Pulling her close, death had stolen her from me. The fire still burned, and my rage was nowhere near ending.

Acid filled my gut, and it felt like lava rolled through my veins. My temples throbbed as the rage and violent creature inside me clawed to escape...Again. This was all my fault. *I should have been here. I never should have left you alone.* I stared into her unblinking eyes and spoke to her through gritted teeth.

"I am so sorry, baby. I always fuck things up. Always let you down. And now...Now."

Tears blinded me and splashed over Inez's face. I pulled her lifeless body against mine and squeezed. Just daring, cursing *death* to come take her from me.

I was goddamn sure I'd fail at that, too.

The desperate cries from Bellia filled my ears; they tore at me like a rusty knife. If I couldn't take care of Inez, how in the hell could I even hope to keep her safe? It's the end of the fucking world out there.

I looked down into Inez's eyes, again.

"Please, baby. Please tell me what to do. You always knew what's best. Tell me how to fix this...shit. My sweetness, I'm begging you, for Christ's sake...Tell me what to do!" I heard myself screaming into her slack face.

She answered. A soft-red glow in her eyes made me jump— almost piss myself.

Her head turned, slowly, hungrily toward me. Her mouth moving and body twitching. I pulled her closer.

"Child of Light?" Inez's undead lips whispered to me, in a voice that was not quite her own. She clawed at my throat as the orange sunlight of dawn bathed her pale face. Even in death she stole my heart.

"Must find...Child of Light...Must...Kill it," she said as she tore at my arms and tried to bite me.

"Child..what the hell?" I fought her off and held her down.

She kept repeating the same thing, over and over again, while trying to make me a fucking happy meal. I felt my tears rolling down my face. The burning in my gut was telling me the dark and sickening truth.

"*Child of Light*...die." She hissed and bit the cold air.

I had no clue what the hell she was talking about, or, how the fuck she was able to talk at all. My instincts still seemed to be with me. I had no idea why. But while my left arm held her down and tears of guilt, sadness, and rage rained from my goddamned face, my right hand found purchase on my Gerber Mark II folding knife inside my boot.

Inez moaned and kept growling about the damn, '*Child of Light*,' shit. I had the knife in my hand.

I held it above her snipping mouth, trying desperately to aim.

My hand shook. I hesitated.

Inez lunged for my throat.

I cried out and watched my arm react—slice down with well-trained reflex reaction. I screamed.

The six-inch blade tore deep into her eye socket, and I could feel her cold blood and flesh splash onto my hand as I pinned her to the floor.

Inez lay still. Grief, self-loathing, and anger swallowed my sorry ass like a dark tide, pulling me down. My body shook with sobs and what blood she had left drained onto the carpet.

Lost.

In the distance I heard something.

It started low at first, and slowly grew louder and shrill.

Crying...A baby crying.

Bellia!

"Ranger!" The word came like a shotgun blast as I awoke.

My head spun, and I turned to the source of the noise.

"Time to put on your big *Ranger* pants, old man. This little girl here needs her daddy." Stacy Jo stood in the hallway with Bellia in her arms. She wore that 'I ain't taking no shit' look on her face.

I spent the next hour burying the love of my life. The one good thing about having a strong, tall palisade fence, it keeps the goddamn *meat-eaters* out. I had two constant companions:

Grief and rage.

They would serve me well.

After all, it was the end of the world. And something told me that this whole Child of Light thing might be important.

I stood with Stacy Jo and baby Bellia looking out the picture window of our house. The tears never stopped, and the pain still burned in my gut.

"What now, old man?" the girl asked as she checked the pistol in her hands.

The morning sun wasn't as warm as usual this time of year, but its rays still covered us in light.

"Hell. Here's what I think. First, I get myself a drink, then we load up the truck with as much shit as it can handle, and we go find out what this whole Child of Light shit is about." I kissed Bellia's forehead and looked out on the cul-de-sac, filled with burned out cars, bodies, and of course... Zombies.

"Sounds good to me, Ranger." Stacy Jo nodded, looking out the window.

166

"Good. Let's do this," was all I said, and handed Bellia to Stacy Jo and headed to the garage. After all, it was the end of the world.

I never could take a damn day off.

-End-

CHECK OUT OTHER GREAT ZOMBIE NOVELS

Z BURBIA
by Jake Bible

Whispering Pines is a classic, quiet, private American subdivision on the edge of Asheville, NC, set in the pristine Blue Ridge Mountains. Which is good since the zombie apocalypse has come to Western North Carolina and really put suburban living to the test!

Surrounded by a sea of the undead, the residents of Whispering Pines have adapted their bucolic life of block parties to scavenging parties, common area groundskeeping to immediate area warfare, neighborhood beautification to neighborhood fortification.

But, even in the best of times, suburban living has its ups and downs what with nosy neighbors, a strict Home Owners' Association, and a property management company that believes the words "strict interpretation" are holy words when applied to the HOA covenants. Now with the zombie apocalypse upon them even those innocuous, daily irritations quickly become dramatic struggles for personal identity, family security, and straight up survival.

ZOMBIE RULES
by David Achord

Zach Gunderson's life sucked and then the zombie apocalypse began.

Rick, an aging Vietnam veteran, alcoholic, and prepper, convinces Zach that the apocalypse is on the horizon. The two of them take refuge at a remote farm. As the zombie plague rages, they face a terrifying fight for survival.

They soon learn however that the walking dead are not the only monsters.

CHECK OUT OTHER GREAT ZOMBIE NOVELS

900 MILES
by S. Johnathan Davis

John is a killer, but that wasn't his day job before the Apocalypse.

In a harrowing 900 mile race against time to get to his wife just as the dead begin to rise, John, a business man trapped in New York, soon learns that the zombies are the least of his worries, as he sees first-hand the horror of what man is capable of with no rules, no consequences and death at every turn.

Teaming up with an ex-army pilot named Kyle, they escape New York only to stumble across a man who says that he has the key to a rumored underground stronghold called Avalon..... Will they find safety? Will they make it to Johns wife before it's too late?

Get ready to follow John and Kyle in this fast paced thriller that mixes zombie horror with gladiator style arena action!

WHITE FLAG OF THE DEAD
by Joseph Talluto

Millions died when the Enillo Virus swept the earth. Millions more were lost when the victims of the plague refused to stay dead, instead rising to slaughter and feed on those left alive. For survivors like John Talon and his son Jake, they are faced with a choice: Do they submit to the dead, raising the white flag of surrender? Or do they find the will to fight, to try and hang on to the last shreds or humanity?

CHECK OUT OTHER GREAT ZOMBIE NOVELS

VACCINATION
by Phillip Tomasso

What if the H7N9 vaccination wasn't just a preventative measure against swine flu?

It seemed like the flu came out of nowhere and yet, in no time at all the government manufactured a vaccination. Were lab workers diligent, or could the virus itself have been man-made? Chase McKinney works as a dispatcher at 9-1-1. Taking emergency calls, it becomes immediately obvious that the entire city is infected with the walking dead. His first goal is to reach and save his two children.

Could the walls built by the U.S.A. to keep out illegal aliens, and the fact the Mexican government could not afford to vaccinate their citizens against the flu, make the southern border the only plausible destination for safety?

ZOMBIE, INC
by Chris Dougherty

"WELCOME! To Zombie, Inc. The United Five State Republic's leading manufacturer of zombie defense systems! In business since 2027, Zombie, Inc. puts YOU first. YOUR safety is our MAIN GOAL! Our many home defense options - from Ze Fence® to Ze Popper® to Ze Shed® - fit every need and every budget. Use Scan Code "TELL ME MORE!" for your FREE, in-home*, no obligation consultation! *Schedule your appointment with the confidence that you will NEVER HAVE TO LEAVE YOUR HOME! It isn't safe out there and we know it better than most! Our sales staff is FULLY TRAINED to handle any and all adversarial encounters with the living and the undead". Twenty-five years after the deadly plague, the United Five State Republic's most successful company, Zombie, Inc., is in trouble. Will a simple case of dwindling supply and lessening demand be the end of them or will Zombie, Inc. find a way, however unpalatable, to survive?

CPSIA information can be obtained at www.ICGtesting.com
Printed in the USA
LVOW04s2141040315

429274LV00034B/1649/P